"He can put a story together that will have you on the edge of your chair. Holden writes in a hard, fast, crisp style and he has a feel for colorful language and characters that makes the story sing."

—*Mammoth Mystery*

"[One of] the real pros of suspense."

—Anthony Boucher,
The New York Times

"... one of those forgotten paperbackers who deserves to be remembered."

—Bill Crider

Dead Wrong

by Lorenz Heller
writing as
Larry Holden

Black Gat Books • Eureka California

DEAD WRONG

Published by Black Gat Books
A division of Stark House Press
1315 H Street
Eureka, CA 95501, USA
griffinskye3@sbcglobal.net
www.starkhousepress.com

ISBN-13: 978-1-951473-03-7

Book design by Jeff Vorzimmer, ¡caliente!design, Austin, Texas
Proofreading by Bill Kelly
Cover art by Rafael DeSoto, 1953

First Stark House Press/Black Gat Edition: June 2020

One

I was expecting Harry Loomis at ten-thirty, which meant he'd turn up anywhere between that time and the boisterous A.M.'s before the bars closed. Or after, or the next day, or maybe he'd get side-tracked with a bottle of bourbon and a fat, willing blonde and wouldn't show up at all and around Tuesday or Wednesday I'd get a call from Hoboken to come down and bail him out on three or four charges, including public drunkenness, disturbing the peace and assault and battery. He was a tough, to-hell-with-it man when he got going on the liquor.

Harry was chief mate on one of the freighters of the Trans-Ocean Line, plying between Port Newark and the West Coast, trading chiefly in lumber from Washington State. I got to know him when I was a light-heavy in the semi-finals at the old Atlas Arena on Frelinghuysen Avenue. One night he came around to the dressing room to pat me on the back and to say he liked a scrapper who wasn't afraid to get in there and mix. He was a fight fan, but I don't think he liked the fights so much as the blood and violence. I was just a kid and nobody had ever come to my dressing room before, so naturally I was flattered.

We did the town that night and I got home a day and a half later with a hangover that should have been taken out and shot, as an act of mercy. After that, he made a point of seeing me every once in a while after his boat docked and some of our toots were hair-raising. For a man in his fifties, he was wild as they came. He was short and wiry, never without a shot-loaded blackjack in his pocket. Some of the guys he picked on, I'm telling you, he scared the living pants off me, but there was always that blackjack in the clutch and many's the time we left a joint at top speed through the back door.

It tapered off after I quit the ring, and in the end we saw each other maybe once or twice a year, which was okay with me. I wasn't a kid anymore and a perambulating two-man riot didn't have the same appeal. In fact, I'd have been just as well pleased to drop the whole thing.

I'd gone into business for myself—the Malone Building Supply Company, a one-man, one-truck outfit—and the competition was rough, really rough. The time was past when I could afford to start the day with a gory-eyed hangover. I had to be on the jump every minute.

I'd wanted to call it off but there had been no way of getting in touch with him after making the date, so I thought, oh hell, once more won't hurt, though I made up my mind then and there this was the last time. You can't mix business with pleasure—if you want to call it pleasure.

I must have dozed—it had been a rugged day—because suddenly the doorbell was ringing and I jumped from the sofa, thinking it was the alarm clock. It took me a minute to realize it was still the same night and not five-thirty in the morning. Yawning and thick-eyed from sleep, I switched on the light. I arranged an unfelt grin of welcome on my face and opened the door with a noisy "Come in, you old—" and put on the brakes. It wasn't Harry.

It was a girl, a tall girl with gray eyes, light brown hair and a nervous smile. She was wearing a green seersucker suit and a white blouse with a little collar that would have been prim on anybody else. The suit looked like a twelve-ninety-five imitation of something the designer had caught a brief glimpse of in a passing Cadillac, but even the cheap tailoring couldn't hide the fact that she had a good, leggy figure underneath, as well as all the other features so dear to the wolfish hearts of the street-corner whistlers. But she was really a sweet, clean-looking girl and had the quality of being unused, earnest and decent. You could tell that when she married a guy it could be for good, not kicks. In short, the kind of girl I knew practically nothing about.

"Sorry, miss," I apologized, "I thought it was somebody else."

She took a tighter hold on her white plastic handbag and said nervously, "Mr.—Malone?"

"That's right. Joe Malone."

"I'm Claire Loomis."

I was so surprised I didn't know what to say. Was she Harry's wife, daughter, cousin or what? But no, she couldn't be Harry's wife, not this girl. A girl would have to be either a broad or out of her mind to marry a guy like him.

I must have stared at her because she said, "Didn't my father tell you about me?"

"Not a word, but maybe he didn't get around to it. His boat just docked this morning. I'm expecting him"—I looked at my watch—"in about a half hour. Do you want to come in and sit down?"

She hesitated and said, "Well—"

"It's okay," I told her. "I won't make a pass at you. Believe it or not, I can act like a gentleman when the time comes."

"I'm sure you can," she said, smiling. "Thank you."

We went in the living room. She sat in the lounge chair and I sat on the sofa and, of the two of us, I was the one who wasn't at my ease. I wasn't used to girls like that. The ones I knew were mutts by comparison. I didn't know whether to offer her a drink, a glass of milk or a cup of coffee.

"I didn't know Harry was married," I said, to start the ball rolling. "And how's he been? I haven't seen him for a year and a half."

"I haven't seen him for twenty years," she said in a low voice.

I said, "Twenty years!" and couldn't think of

anything to add. What *can* you say?

"He and my mother were separated when I was four," she said.

There was no answer to that one either. I didn't want to sit there like a dummy, so I asked her if she'd like a drink.

"I got applejack," I said. "It's good stuff. You won't strangle. Or you can have ginger ale. I got that, too."

"Applejack? I've never had it."

"It tastes like apples. I drink it straight or with club soda."

"With club soda, thank you."

I made two mild ones, hoping it would loosen me up a bit. Otherwise it was going to be a painful half-hour. I never had any trouble entertaining girls; but I didn't know what to say to this one, and I certainly wasn't going to tell her any dirty jokes. I passed out the drinks and she took a sip.

"It does taste like apples," she said.

"Yeah, that's what they make it from."

"It's very good."

"I like it myself. You live around here, Miss Loomis?"

"I'm from Columbus, Ohio."

"I've never been there. How is it?"

"Very pleasant."

"There's some nice parts in Newark, too, but I like it better out in the country."

I was doing fine with this brilliant conversation. She'd certainly never forget Joe Malone. When she got back to Columbus she could tell all her friends about the fascinating moron she met in Newark. I really wanted to make an impression on her, but not this kind. I felt like Dummy Stuss, the deaf and dumb newsie who had the stand near City Hall.

But in the back of my mind was the nagging question: Why had Harry told her to come here? This was no place for a family reunion. And that led to other questions. Why was Harry coming here himself? We usually met in Patsy's Bar on Market Street around six in the evening, never this late. There was nothing for a chief mate to do aboard the boat till ten at night, especially in the home port. It was a funny situation all round. I knew it would be cleared up when Loomis came, but in the meantime it was worse than a wake, in addition to my not knowing the score.

I looked at Claire and smiled stiffly, the way you do when the silence becomes a congestion. We had talked about applejack. It tasted like apples. We had talked about geography, Columbus and Newark. What next? The weather. We could always swap the weather. Maybe they had a very interesting climate in Ohio. In Newark, the winters were cold and rainy and the summers were hot and rainy, especially on weekends.

I was saved by the bell. Literally. The telephone bell. I jumped up, crossing my fingers that it was Harry. It was.

"Hi, kid," he said, "what's on your mind? The watchman said for me to call you."

The watchman. A wonderful guy. He was a real gentleman and I owed him an apology. I had phoned Trans-Ocean earlier in the evening to call off the date and the watchman had been a real stinker.

"Nobody here," he had said grouchily. "They all went home for the day. There's nobody aboard the boats."

"I know he's aboard. He sent me a note saying he'd be there till ten. I have to get in touch with him. It's important."

"Sorry, but I can't go traipsing down to the docks."

"Damn it, I have to talk to him."

"Don't yell at me, young feller. I don't have to take your guff."

He was a stubborn, crabby, self-important old goat. He made me sore, but I knew the type—he'd hang up if I crossed him. I calmed down.

"All right," I said. "Will you give him message?"

"I ain't guaranteeing nothing."

"Tell him to call Joe Malone. Malone—M-a-l-o-n-e. Essex Nine, three one three one."

"I can spell, mister."

I said, "Ah, go to hell," and hung up.

But apparently he'd had a change of heart and had given Harry the message after all.

"Oh yeah," I said, "About tonight. I can't make it. I'm in business for myself now and have to get up at five-thirty."

"You're not sore at me, are you, kid?"

"I'm not sore. I have to get to bed early, that's all."

"You sounded sore. I don't want you to be sore at me, Kid."

This wasn't like Harry at all. He seemed worried and anxious to pacify me and he actually stammered as if he had the jitters.

"Nothing like that, Harry," I said. "It's just I can't drive a truck with a hangover."

"Sure, sure, kid, that's okay. I didn't feel like going on a binge anyway." Then in a low, hurried voice, "You get my note and stuff?"

"Sure. Your daughter's here, by the way."

"Oh for crissake!" he swore savagely. "Listen, get rid of her. Tell her to go back to the hotel. I'll see her tomorrow."

"The hell with that."

"Tell her to beat it. I can't be bothered with her tonight."

After twenty years, he couldn't be bothered with her tonight!

"Don't be a louse," I said sharply. "She's been waiting for you and I'm not going to boot her out."

"But I can't see her tonight, kid. Brush her off. You know how to do it. Let her down easy. Say I'll take her out to lunch tomorrow."

"Okay," I said flatly. "In that case, don't bother coming around yourself. I'm going to bed."

"Wait a minute, kid, now just a minute. Don't blow off. Let her stay. I'll talk to her when I get there."

"Don't you want to say hello to her now?"

"It can wait. I'll see both of you in about a half-hour. You're not sore at me now, are you, Joe?"

"I'm nuts about you," I growled, and hung up.

Now I was in a kind of fix. It bothered me, but I didn't worry about it. Harry had asked about his "stuff"—and there wasn't any stuff. A big drunken sailor—whose name turned out to be Jeff Buckley—had been bumbling around my apartment when I got home at six. I seldom keep the door locked. There's nothing to steal. He had a note from Harry and had been all day delivering it, having spent considerable time in the cheap-drink bars on Market Street. In fact, he was so soused he'd almost forgotten he had a note for me.

The note said, Hi, Joe—just docked but I'll be stuck here till ten or so tonight. See you then. Here's a little present for you. Keep it till I come and I'll show you some tricks, ha, ha, Harry.

And that was it. There wasn't any present. Buckley had lost it or given it away or God knows what, and he hadn't the faintest remembrance of it. But I honestly didn't care. Harry's idea of a little present was a package of itching powder that sprayed your hands when you opened it or a baby alligator that tried to bite your finger off. I could do without his little presents.

So instead of raising Cain with the big dumb rummy of a sailor, I wrote a note to Harry and put it in the same envelope he had addressed to me: *Hi, Harry—see you about ten-thirty. I could use a little excitement. Thanks for the present. It was a real yak, as usual. Joe.*

So there was Harry asking about the present and

there wasn't any. But nuts. I'd tell him it fell out the window or I gave it to the janitor's kid. I was frankly more worried about Claire Loomis than one of her father's custard-pie presents.

I turned from the phone and she was looking at me gravely, her eyes troubled. She had been sitting there all the time and had overheard everything. I turned fire-engine red.

"I shouldn't have come," she said in a low voice, not looking at me.

"But if he told you—"

"But he didn't really, you see. He said he'd get in touch with me at the hotel. He didn't say to come here tonight."

I said, "Oh," and wondered what was going on. I didn't understand any of it.

"Don't be angry with him," she pleaded. "It's not his fault, and he hasn't been well."

"He didn't sound like himself," I admitted.

"He's worried, too."

"I got that impression."

She didn't say any more, and I could see she was embarrassed both from Harry's having made a fuss and her being here unexpectedly. Also, she was a little worried, herself. She was a nice kid and I felt sorry for her. I don't know what she was expecting after twenty years, but Harry certainly wasn't going to be it. In fact, as a father, he was going to be quite a shock.

She put her glass on the little table beside the chair and picked up her purse. "I think I'd better go back to the hotel," she said in a small voice.

I wanted her to stay. I had the feeling that if I let her go then, I'd never see her again and suddenly it was important to make friends with her. She was genuinely special in a deep, warm way and I had the notion that, under the proper circumstances she could make a man feel special too. She had real quality.

"There's no reason to go," I said quickly. "He's expecting to see you here now."

It seemed ages before she sank back in her chair again. "You're very nice," she murmured.

I knew damn well I wasn't but for a minute she made me think I could learn how.

"Let's look at the TV," I suggested. "It'll help pass the time."

I switched it on and got a program about underwater fishing in the Bahamas. Ordinarily I'd have tuned in to the fights or wrestling, but I didn't think she'd go for a couple guys mauling each other around, so we looked at the fish and it turned out to be very interesting. Following that was an old film with Irene Dunne and Fred MacMurray, a comedy, one of those silly things with people misunderstanding each other and almost marrying somebody else till a grouchy old dame with a heart of gold stepped in and set everything right. A stinker.

The clock crawled around to ten-thirty, then eleven o'clock, then eleven-thirty and still no Loomis. We were both beginning to look at our wristwatches every two minutes.

"I don't know what's holding him up," I said. "He should have been here an hour ago."

It was the wrong thing to say and I kicked myself the moment it was out of my mouth. I knew she was worried.

"He said definitely he was coming?" she asked, her hands a tight bundle in her lap.

"Well, yes—but it wouldn't be the first time he got interested in something else. Harry kind of likes to cut loose when he hits port after a long trip."

"But he's sick."

"Sailors are sailors," I said, making a joke of it. "They like to make the rounds. It's practically a law."

"Perhaps we should call the steamship line again."

I didn't feel much like talking to that crabby watchman again, but if it would make her feel easier, I'd have called the FBI. I phoned Trans-Ocean.

"Did Chief Mate Loomis leave yet?" I asked.

The watchman said sourly, "Hold on," and a few seconds later I heard him talking into another phone. He came back. "He didn't go out the gate."

"He has to go out that way?"

"It's the only way out, mister. Everybody goes through the gate. There's no sense calling me no more, mister. I got my own work."

I said thanks and looked at the girl and shrugged. "He must still be tied up on the boat. He didn't check out at the gate."

"You—you don't think anything's wrong, do you?" she asked anxiously.

I didn't know the first thing about the duties of a chief mate on a freighter, but I said, "He probably had to catch up with the paper work. A boat carries a lot of cargo and it takes bookkeeping, especially at the end of a trip. Everything has to balance. It's a business like any other."

It sounded good and she looked relieved. I made two more drinks and we looked at a film about the bears in Yellowstone National Park on TV. We talked a little about my business and her job out in Columbus. She worked in a book store that also sold greeting cards, art supplies, gifts and phonograph records. She had the record department and said it was a lot of fun because she liked music. By music I thought she meant all that gloomy stuff by Beethoven, but it turned out she was crazy about Lunceford, Dorsey, Ellington, Miller and all those guys who played the really good hot stuff. She liked dancing, swimming and boating and I began to see how a guy could have a really good time with her and not have to stand around and respect her every minute, like a queen or a princess, if you know what I mean.

But no matter how much we talked or watched TV we couldn't stop the clock. By twelve-thirty we both knew Harry wasn't going to show up. She couldn't hide her worry any longer. She hadn't seen Loomis for twenty years, so you know how she felt, and I didn't feel so good watching her torment herself. It might have made things easier if I had told her the kind of guy Harry was, but you had to draw the line somewhere. You just didn't tell a girl her father was a bastard even though it might explain the way he was acting. You had to let her find out for herself and make up her own mind. Anyway, it would be too much like squealing.

"Would—would you mind reading his letter?" she asked. "I'd like to see what you think. Perhaps I'm upsetting myself unnecessarily."

She got the letter out of her purse. Her hands were shaking. The letter was written on several sheets of blue-lined paper, the kind you tear out of a pad, and it was full of fine wrinkles as if it had been read, reread and reread again.

Dear Kiddo—

I'll bet this is a shock hearing from your old man after all these years but I been thinking about you. I still have your address from the time you wrote me your mother died two years ago. I meant to answer but things kept coming up. I don't blame you if you don't think of me like your father no more. I know I didn't treat you and your mother right but try to keep it in mind there's two sides to everything and maybe it wasn't all my fault. Your mother probably told you lots of things about me and some of them are true and some aint. It all goes back to we shouldn't have got married in the first place, me working the boats and her wanting a home, we got along like cats and dogs. But I aint denying I should of been a better father and sent your mother some $$$$$ from time to time.

Right now I'm working for the Trans-Ocean Line on the Tranoco, first mate, not bad, hey, kiddo? Trans-Ocean is the one with the green flag and the red T, they call it the hungry T Line on account of the food didn't used to be so good, it's okay now, that was a long time ago and officers eat better anyways, trust the bosses to get the best. And me, I'm a guy I like to eat good, ha, ha.

But something's come up and that's why I'm writing you. I aint been feeling so good. I thought it was rheumatism and went to this doc in Frisco for medicine and he gave me the bad news, arthritis. I'm getting bumps on my joints and it's worse all the time. Deformed arthritis he called it and I got to give up working the boats or end up a cripple. Sometimes it takes me fifteen, twenty minutes to get out of the sack, I'm all stiff and the pain is pretty bad and times I can't use my hands and walk with a limp. I told the captain I fell and wrenched my back or I'd of been out of a job before this, they don't want a first mate that can't get around, he's in charge if something happens to the captain.

It don't hurt so much after four or five drinks but you can't keep lickered up all the time, it gets you, and anyways the doc says lay off the licker, it's the worst thing for you. I'm telling you, kiddo, I never thought I'd end up a cripple and the pain is something fierce, specially after you lay down and get stiff and some nights I have to sleep sitting up, you just can't get comfortable. Maybe they ought to take me out and shoot me like a horse, sometimes I wish they would, the pain. I guess I'm a sissy, kiddo, but it goes on all the time.

I thought it was the end for sure. Working the boats is all I know and I can't go on for another trip and get away with it, they'll catch wise.

But every cloud's got a silver lining, kiddo, and mine came through. I fell into a deal with some guys, an investment, just in the nick of time, and I'll be getting a nice piece of $$$$$ at the end of this trip, so I can quit the boats and get cured, I don't want to be a cripple, and the doc says it's for sure unless I quit the boats and lay off the licker. I been asking around on the sly and everybody says Florida's the place for arthritis and now I'm going to have the $$$$$, just dumb luck. I don't want to be a cripple, kiddo. It'd kill me, being a burden on me and everybody else, but Florida'll fix me up.

Now here's what I thought, kiddo. When this deal comes through, I'll be fixed for life. We can get a little place in Florida and I want you along with me, you're my own flesh and blood. I'm going to be sick for awhile, I need somebody to help me out, but six months or a year be good as new. I know I aint got no right asking you like this after all these years but you're still my daughter and strangers are never the same.

And I'm going to make it up to you, kiddo. You'll have all the $$$$$ you want and I'm fixing it so you get the rest after I kick off, I aint so young no more, fifty-three, I don't look it. Everybody takes me for in the forties. But honest to God, kiddo, give me a hand and you'll never be sorry, I need you. Don't say no right off the bat, think it over, I'm on the level.

I'm sick and I don't want to go in a hospital, they don't give a damn. There's nothing like your own flesh and blood.

Here's $75, all I can scrape up now. Take a train to Newark, N. J. and stay at the National Hotel on High Street. It don't look like much, I wish I could do better, but it's clean and they won't steal you blind like some I can name, $5 a night, no flea bag.

I'll see you after the boat docks in Port Newark. If I miss you or can't make it for some reason, get in touch with a friend of mine, Joe Malone, 732 Mt. Greylock Avenue, Newark. He's a tough mick but in some ways a soft touch and a right guy. I'm sending him something, telling him it's a little present, but it's for you in case I don't show up. He'll give it to you if you show him this letter. Look inside. I want you to have it.

I know I been a louse but I'm telling you the truth, kiddo, I'm one sick guy and you're all I got left. I been thinking about you a lot these days and want to do you right, you can bank on that.

Your father,

Harry C. Loomis

PS—Don't tell nobody about this but Joe Malone, it might be bad. He's on the up and up.

The writing was so scrawly it looked as if he had written it with boxing gloves, but I knew what arthritis can do to your hands. They had to retire Sergeant Vince Elwood down in the precinct on account of it. He still walks with a cane.

But the letter itself was what got me. I never thought I'd see the day when Harry Loomis would weep and whine like that. I didn't blame him for feeling low—arthritis is rough—but he didn't have to moan and beg for sympathy.

What really teed me off, though, was that business about an "investment." Loomis had never invested in anything but a good time for himself, liquor and the dames. He was just handing Claire a line to get her to take care of him. Maybe he did have a few hundred bucks, but I'd give odds he was depending on her getting a job after his money was gone. It made me sick to my stomach, the son of a bitch.

She was watching me tensely, waiting to hear what I'd have to say, but I couldn't tell her what I thought. Anyway, there was an outside chance Loomis did have something lined up.

"Well," I said lamely, "I still don't think you have anything to worry about."

"But he's so sick," she protested.

And scared witless, I thought.

"Sure," I said, "but he tells you right here it helps if he takes four or five drinks when the pain gets bad. He might have taken seven or eight and fell asleep in his bunk."

"But—aren't there dangerous places on a boat? I mean, a man with arthritis could fall and hurt himself and if he's alone, he wouldn't be found until morning."

I thought of the open holds. The hatches would be off. If he fell into one of those, it wouldn't make any difference when they found him. It would be like falling out of a second-story window onto an iron-plated sidewalk. But there were other places he could fall, down a companionway or off the gangplank to the dock, and if nobody was around, he could be in trouble.

"We'll take a run out there," I said. "Maybe we can talk ourselves inside for a look around."

She said, "Thanks, Joe," and her voice was warm with gratitude, which made me feel worse because I wasn't doing her a favor, helping her to get mixed up with Harry Loomis.

We took my car and were out there in a half-hour. The gate area was floodlighted, which blacked out everything beyond, but I knew what it looked like—big warehouses, boats with booms sticking up like dead trees, and lumber and other non-perishable cargo stacked up all over the docks. A heavy wire mesh fence surrounded the area, and it was topped by five strands of barbed wire on a frame that stuck out over the road at a forty-five-degree angle. As we parked the car, the gateman came out of a little shack. He had on a tan uniform and was wearing a gun.

"What do you want here?" he demanded.

First I asked if Harry had come out yet and he said no, then I went into the pitch about waiting for him since ten-thirty and he was sick and we were afraid he had taken a fall and hurt himself, but I wasn't getting any place till Claire stepped in.

"He's my father," she said, "and he really is sick. We're worried."

The gateman shook his head. "I can't let you in, miss, unless you work here."

He didn't visibly soften, but I could tell he was thinking it over. We talked some more and he kept saying it was against the rules and the company was stricter because there had been some robberies and he wished he could do something but rules were rules. I showed him my driver's license and he said, "Oh, you're the fella he called around ten o'clock." I said yes and gave him a business card that said Malone Building Supply Company, and Claire showed him her license and the envelope of Loomis' letter with his name up in the corner and the return address of the Trans-Ocean Line under it. He must have been looking for an excuse to let us in by that time because he studied the envelope and finally nodded.

"Okay," he said, "I guess I can take a chance, being you're a member of the family, miss, but it's against the rules all the same."

With that off his chest, he relaxed and turned out to be a nice guy. He unlocked the big gate and let us in and said he'd drive us down to the dock in the jeep.

"I've known Harry for years," he said. "Always good for a laugh, the stories he told, but I didn't think he looked so good tonight. Something on his mind, I thought. He was expecting somebody else tonight, too."

"I wouldn't know anything about that," I said.

"Yeah. I saw him four or five times when I made the rounds, and he kept wanting to know if anybody'd been around asking for him. Your call was the only one, though."

A thin moon floated hazily and the boat was a high, jagged silhouette against the sky. A naked electric light bulb burned at the head of the gangplank, and a man in an officer's cap leaned against the rail, smoking a pipe. He waved when the jeep stopped on the dock. The gateman called up to him.

"Hi there, Mr. Groff. Is Harry Loomis still aboard?" And in an aside, he added to us, "Mr. Groff is the third mate."

Groff took the pipe from his mouth. "The Chief? He left about quarter after ten."

"You sure? He was supposed to meet these folks at ten-thirty and hasn't shown up. They're worried. This is Harry's daughter."

"Well no, I'm not sure. I was in my cabin studying"—he held up a book,—"and he stopped at the door and said so long and I thought he went."

"Maybe we better come aboard and take a look. Miss Loomis said he was sick and might have fallen down some place."

Groff said, "Oh God!" Then, "I'll get a flashlight."

We walked up the steep gangplank and I saw, to my relief, that the holds were still covered. A fall into one of those pits would have finished him for sure.

Lumber was still piled on the decks. The gateman had a flashlight, too, and we went over the boat from bow to stern. It was pretty eerie the way the black shadows kept jumping away from the flashlight beams and everything so quiet except for our footsteps and the lap-lap-lap of the uneasy water against the hull. We looked in the fo'c'sle, the officers' staterooms, the galley, the sick bay, the radio shack, down into the silent engine rooms and even into the paint lockers and chain lockers. We made a slow, thorough job of it, afraid every minute that we'd find a huddled body at the foot of a companionway. In his cabin we found a half-filled bottle of rye, some clothes and a sextant in his locker and a pair of binoculars hanging by a strap from a hook in the door, but there was no other sign of him aboard. We hardly exchanged a word till we stood at the gangplank again in the light of the harsh naked bulb that made us all look gaunt and hollow-eyed. In a way, I wished we had found Harry with something minor, like a mild concussion, to end the suspense.

"Could he have gotten out without your seeing him?" I asked the gateman.

"Well"—he glanced toward the brightly lighted gate—"he might have climbed the fence. He was an impatient guy and if I was making the rounds he might have done that. What was he doing here so late anyway?" he asked Groff. "He don't usually hang around any longer than he has to."

"He wasn't doing anything as far as I could see," said Groff. "Mostly he sat up on the bridge smoking cigarettes. I tried to talk to him a few times but he just grunted, so I left him alone. Come to think of it, he had an argument with somebody on the dock around nine-thirty."

The gateman said, "Nine-thirty. That could have been Jeff Buckley. He came in around that time, drunk."

"That was it. The Chief called him a dumb rummy—among other things." Groff grinned. He was about twenty-five and looked Scandinavian with his blond hair, high cheekbones and tilted, wide-nostriled nose. "Gave him merry hell. What happened to Buckley? He go out again?"

"Yeah," the gateman nodded. "I told him to go some place and sleep it off. I'm sorry we couldn't find your father, miss, but it's my guess he climbed the fence. That'd be Harry's style, right, Mr. Groff?"

"If you were making the rounds, he wouldn't wait," Groff agreed.

"Thanks for everything you've done," Claire said wanly. "I'm sorry to have put you to all this trouble."

The gateman drove us back in the jeep and we thanked him again when he let us out. Claire walked silently to the car beside me. By this time she must have been getting a pretty good idea of what Harry was like.

"Well take one more look at my apartment," I said. "He might have gone there while we were here."

"But you really don't think so, do you?"

"There's always the chance," I evaded.

"You think he went to a bar, don't you? Or several bars. That would have been his style, wouldn't it?"

"Let's try my apartment before making any guesses."

It was useless and I knew it, but I wanted to give Harry every chance, for Claire's sake. He wasn't at my place and that was the end of the line for us. He could have been in any of the hundreds of gin mills between here and Hoboken, a drink in his hand and his arm around the first willing dame he came to.

"I'd better go back to the hotel," Claire said heavily. "There's not much use looking further, is there?"

"Not much. He'll probably turn up in the morning."

Or the morning after or next week, depending on how much of a load he tied on. Claire understood that now without my having to tell her. I drove her to her hotel on High Street, a gloomy pile of red brick with a lobby like a cave, a lousy place for Harry to have sent her—though better than the flophouses on Mulberry Street.

"You've been wonderful, Joe," she said when I took her to the door. "You've been very patient."

"He's a friend," I said. "I wanted to make sure he's all right."

"Call me tomorrow."

"I sure will. I have to go to Trenton pretty early, but I'll call the minute I get back."

"Please do."

I had a good feeling as I drove away, as if something significant had taken place that night. I was sore at Harry for having gone off on a bat at a time like this, but that faded to unimportance when I thought of Claire. I'd never have gotten to know her if he hadn't pulled his wingding. I was humming under my breath as I trotted up the stairs to my apartment. I opened the door and caught a brief, incredible glimpse of a guy swinging toward me. I yelled and tried to throw up my hands but something thunked against my head and blackness came up with a roar.

Two

When I opened my eyes, I was lying on the hall floor and half the neighbors were standing around in pajamas and house-coats. Kubec, the guy from the next apartment, was kneeling and holding a bottle of ammonia to my nose. I gagged and pushed it away.

"Wha—what happened?" I asked thickly.

The neighbors looked at each other as if I were drunk and Kubec said, "I heard you yell and when I came out you were laying on the floor."

I sat up dizzily and he put his arm around me. "All right, all right," he growled at the others. "Go to bed. The show's over. Matinee tomorrow afternoon."

He helped me into the apartment and closed the door with his foot. "Them jerks," he grumbled. "You'd think they never took a drink in their life. They give me a—for the love of Pete!"

He stared incredulously around the room and dully, still hanging on his arm, I did the same. The place was a mess. My clothes had been pulled out of the closet and thrown all over the floor, the sofa-bed was pulled out from the wall, the lounge chair was overturned and the bottom ripped open, and even the drawers of my desk had been jerked out and emptied in a pile on the rug. It wasn't till then that I remembered the guy swinging on me when I opened the door. I remembered his buck teeth and the savage expression on his face and his arm coming down before I could get my hands up. There had been something familiar about him but I couldn't think what.

"I walked in on him," I told Kubec.

He swore. "A couple seconds quicker and I'd have caught the son of a bitch!"

I touched my head gingerly. There was a small, uncut lump over my left ear. "Maybe you were lucky," I said. "He had a blackjack."

"I'd have stuffed it down his throat. Want me to call the cops, Malone?"

I didn't want the cops. It was after three now and if they came I wouldn't get to bed at all.

"Forget it," I said. "He didn't get anything. There wasn't anything to get. Can I give you a drink?"

"I better not. You sure you're okay? How's the head?"

"I've had worse on beer."

He laughed. "Me, too. Too bad we didn't catch that bastard, but he must have been pretty dumb, pulling a robbery in this lousy neighborhood. Ain't none of us got nothing worth carrying down the stairs."

He wanted to stand around and talk about it but I eased him out. I was grateful for his help but I had to get some sleep. I left the apartment the way it was, set the alarm for five-thirty and fell into bed.

Ten seconds later, it seemed, the bell was screaming in my ear and I rolled out of bed, slapping groggily at the clock to shut it off. I had a headache too big for my skull and for a while felt worse than if I hadn't gotten any sleep at all. Fifteen minutes later I was in the truck and on the road to Trenton. I had breakfast with three cups of coffee in New Brunswick on Route 142, and rolled up to the loading platform of Trenton Floor & Tile at eight on the dot. The headache had subsided to a dull thudding that pulsed with my heartbeat, and I'd stopped wincing every tune I blinked my eyes. It wasn't any worse now than an average hangover. There were two trucks ahead of me and I didn't get loaded till after nine. The standing around made me dopey and I picked up some caffeine pills in the drug store before I started back. All in all, it was nearly noon when I rolled into Newark again.

I called Claire from the first phone I came to and it was a definite disappointment when the clerk told me she wasn't in.

"Did she leave word when she'll be back?" I asked.

"No, she didn't, sir. I'm sorry. Would you care to leave a message?"

"Yeah, tell her Joe Malone called."

"Joe Malone? Yes, sir. Thank you." He had an old voice like somebody's tired grandfather.

I delivered the tile to the contractor in North Arlington and tried to promote some more business from him but the best I could get was an order for thirty rolls of tarpaper. He needed more stuff, he said, but he had to unload the two completed houses in which his money was tied up.

"I'll tell you who might be in the market," he said. "My brother-in-law and his partner. They're putting up some bungalows on the west side of Nutley, the Essex Gardens development. I'll give them a ring and say you're coming."

I had lunch in the diner on Ridge Road, and called Claire again. She was still out, so I went over to Nutley. I was beginning to drag my caboose and didn't feel much like talking business, but when you're on your own there's no such thing as goofing off unless you want to start working for somebody else again. Later I was tickled to death I hadn't obeyed that impulse to go home and lie down and take a nice long nap till next Sunday or Monday. The boys in Nutley were working on a close margin and were delighted with the prices I could quote them, which was between ten and twenty per cent under market. I walked out with a nice order for galvanized leader and gutters, ten bathtubs I had that had been slightly damaged in shipping but not enough to show, a thousand feet of conduit and a load of shingles. If I'd been a day earlier I could have sold them a lot of other stuff, but they promised to keep me in mind for a development they had their eye on in Rutherford.

I had to go to Hoboken for the leader and gutters. The Hudson Sheet Metal Works was going out of business and was selling the stuff almost at cost to get rid of it, which was fine for the builders and me.

I kept calling Claire's hotel but she hadn't come back. "She was expecting her father," I told the clerk. "Do you know if he showed up or not?"

"I really wouldn't know, sir. Is this Mr. Malone?"

"Yeah, it's still Malone."

"Er—where are you now, Mr. Malone?"

I thought that a funny question but said, "No place she can reach me. I'm on the road."

"I thought, well, if she came in she might want to telephone you."

"Tell her she can get me at my place around six, but I'll call back in the meantime."

"I'll tell her that, sir. Does she know where to reach you?"

"Sure. Mount Greylock Avenue. She knows."

"Mount Greylock Avenue?"

Now he had gone past the ordinary clerkly desire for information and was starting to sound nosy, so I said shortly, "Don't bother taking it down. I'll call her."

I went back to the truck. Well, Loomis had shown up and he and Claire were taking in the sights, which must have been a new experience for Harry. Acting like a father, I mean. Still, I hadn't seen him for a year and a half and he might have changed. I wanted to give him the benefit of the doubt, for Claire's sake. But I didn't understand her not leaving word for me. She had asked me to call. I finished work at quarter of six and phoned again but she hadn't come back, which put a damper on things because I had counted on seeing her that night. I didn't want to think she was giving me the brushoff, but that's what it amounted to.

Three

Kubec and Bivens, the janitor, were talking on the sidewalk when I drove the truck into the empty lot behind the apartment house, and both started toward me the minute I made the turn. There was a quickness in their step that said plainly they weren't coming to pass the time of day. Bivens was the first.

"The police were here looking for you, Mr. Malone."

"But don't blame me," Kubec said hurriedly. "I didn't say nothing about it, the robbery. It must have been one of the women. You know what they are."

"What'd they want?" I asked Bivens.

"Just when you'd be home, is all. And a couple other things like what kind of tenant are you and did you throw wild parties and all that. I said you never gave me no trouble."

"Did they ask about the robbery?"

"Nope, and I didn't say nothing neither. I figured that was your business. I told them you usually got in after six."

"It wasn't me," Kubec insisted. "I didn't tell nobody but the wife."

Which was the same as putting it on TV in Technicolor—but I didn't make any remarks.

Bivens wasn't finished. "And two other fellas was here, too," he said.

"Not cops?"

"Friends of yours, they said."

"Friends? Was one of them small and thin with a long jaw?" I asked, describing Harry Loomis.

"He might have stayed in the car. I talked to the other one, a kind of foreigner, he looked. Dark. He wanted to know where to locate you and I said Malone Building Supplies but I didn't know the address. They didn't give their name or say they'd be back. They get in touch with you?"

"I've been on the road all day."

"It wasn't me that called the cops," Kubec told me again. "I wouldn't do a thing like that."

I told him it wasn't a catastrophe and went upstairs. I groaned when I saw the mess. I had almost forgotten I hadn't cleaned it up. I was wearily hanging the clothes back in the closet when the knock came on the door. I muttered, "Cops," in a resigned voice and went to answer it. There were two of them, one heavy and stolid, obviously a cop in plain clothes, the other a hard, compact man, about five foot ten, with sandy hair and eyes the remote color of the horizon on a January morning when you're driving down the highway toward Perth Amboy before breakfast.

He showed a gold badge in the palm of his hand and said, "Lieutenant Flavin, homicide. This is Sergeant Gilman. Are you Joe Malone?"

"That's right," I said, the word homicide giving me a shock.

I stepped aside and let them in. Flavin looked at the chaos, then quickly at me.

"Had some trouble, Malone?" he asked.

I shrugged. "Attempted robbery last night."

He lifted his eyebrows and looked around the room again, "They really tore things up."

"Amateurs," said Gilman woodenly.

"Did you report it?" Flavin asked.

"No, I didn't—"

"Why not?"

"I don't have anything worth taking. Anyway, it was late and I was tired."

"What time was it?"

"Three A.M. or so."

"And they didn't take anything?"

"It was just one guy and he didn't have time. I walked in on him."

"You actually saw him?"

"For about a half second before he socked me. He was a big guy with buck teeth."

"You saw the man, you can describe him, and yet you didn't report it. Why not? You have a phone."

"I just told you. I was tired and had to get up at five-thirty to go to Trenton. I needed the sleep."

"Why are you getting so excited?"

"I'm not excited. I'm trying to tell you why I didn't report it, that's all."

"Don't you know you're supposed to report things like that for the protection of others, especially when you can furnish a description of the burglar? We don't get many burglaries in this neighborhood, do we, Sergeant?"

"Not many. We've had seven or eight muggings, though."

"Look," I said to Flavin, "do you think I'm giving you a line?"

"You could be."

"But why should I?"

"I wouldn't know. It's not my department. But the next time you have a robbery, report it immediately. Let's sit down."

He righted the lounge chair and sat on the arm. Sergeant took a solid position near the door, looking as if he could stand there forever. I sat on the sofa and lit a cigarette. My heart was pumping a little faster. In the flood of questions I had forgotten these boys were from homicide, and now it came back to me. Homicide has a chilling sound and Flavin was just the boy to make it chillier. His eyes were gray nailheads.

"What we came for," he said, lighting a cigarette of his own and letting the smoke drift upward from his mouth like a veil, "is something else again. You were a friend of Harry Loomis, weren't you?"

My stomach turned over and I sat very still. My first thought was, *Harry killed somebody*. "I know him," I said carefully.

"Harry Loomis was found dead this morning around eight o'clock with a fractured skull, a broken jaw and severe lacerations about the head and face. The body was in the weeds two hundred feet or so south of the Trans-Ocean Line fence beside the road." Flavin's voice wasn't exactly casual but from the way he spoke you'd have thought he was describing the war memorial in Military Park across the street from Kresge's Department Store.

"He's dead?" I asked stupidly.

"Yes, he's dead. According to the medical report, he was killed between eleven and twelve last night."

His eyes became suddenly intent as if he were expecting me to blurt out an alibi, but all I felt was sick. If Harry had killed somebody, there might have been what they call extenuating circumstances and he could have gotten out of it, but there was no getting out of this. There's no such thing as un-killing a guy. When he's dead, there's nothing you can do but bury him. Oh Christ, I thought, poor Claire!

"Who—who did it?" I stammered, another dumb question. They wouldn't be here if they knew.

Flavin lifted one shoulder and let it fall. "We'll find out. When was the last time you saw Loomis?"

"About a year and a half ago."

"You didn't see him last night?"

"No."

He took a piece of paper from his inside coat pocket and handed it to me. "Did you write this?"

It was the note I had sent to Harry by Jeff Buckley. "Yes—"

"You say in there you'd see him after ten last night," Flavin interrupted. "You made the date."

"No, he was supposed to come here. Wait a minute—" I went through my pockets but couldn't find the original note from Harry.

"What are you looking for?" Flavin asked.

"A note from Loomis. He made the date to meet

me here."

"Why?"

"I don't know. He wanted to go out on the town, I thought."

"Didn't you think it kind of funny after not seeing him for a year and a half?"

"No, I never saw much of him. Once or twice a year at the most. He was always off some place on the boats—the West Coast, Mexico, South America, Europe."

"Why were you so anxious to see him last night?"

"I wasn't. I mean, after I wrote the note I remembered I had to get up early and—"

"You called him twice at Trans-Ocean and drove out there at one o'clock this morning. That sounds anxious to me."

He had it all wrong and it was urgent to correct him before the thing got out of hand. "It wasn't like that. I—"

"Furthermore, the watchman said you were sore about something and kept telling him it was important for you to see Loomis. What about that?"

I knew I had to keep my temper. This Flavin was a rough man. He kept coming at you from all angles and never let up. He came fast and didn't let you get set. The only thing you could do was keep a tight guard and not blow your stack.

"The first time I called him," I said heavily, "was to break the date. I didn't want to drive to Trenton with a hangover. He called back and said he'd see me around ten-thirty but didn't want to go out on a binge so I said okay. He didn't show, so I called back around eleven-thirty and the watchman said he hadn't left. That was all there was to the phone calls."

"What were you sore about?"

"Because the goddam watchman was snotty."

"Why did you say it was important to see Loomis?"

I held on my patience with both hands. "I wanted

to break the date," I said. "I'm in the building supply business and I had to be in Trenton early to pick up a load of tile. You can check with Trenton Floor & Tile, if you want."

"But Loomis thought you were sore, too, the watchman said. Loomis kept asking you not to be sore at him. Why was that?"

"Because," I said, almost grinding my teeth, "I wanted to break the date. He thought I was sore because I didn't want to go out on a binge with him. I wasn't sore."

"The watchman said Loomis kept begging you not to be mad at him. There was quite a conversation, he said. Was it all about this same date?"

"I—wasn't—sore," I repeated, hoping that if I said it often enough, he'd let up.

And then he surprised me by dropping it and coming in on a different tack. "Is Miss Loomis an old friend, too? Miss Claire Loomis."

His bringing up Claire's name like that acted as a brake and I took a tighter grip on myself. I needed to; he had me going. "I met her last night for the first time," I said.

His eyebrows went up. "You met her for the first time—yet you drove all the way out to Port Newark at one this morning with her when you, yourself, according to your story, were aching to get to bed because you had to get up at five-thirty and drive to Trenton? That doesn't make sense, Malone. You don't do things like that for a total stranger."

"For God's sake!" I said. "The poor kid was upset because her old man hadn't gotten in touch with her. What was I supposed to do, tell her to go to hell?"

"She hadn't seen her father for some time, had she?"

"Twenty years, she said."

Gilman kept looking at me and looking at me, but maybe that was part of the technique to make me nervous. I was nervous, all right, and hoped it didn't show. I was nervous because it was obvious now that they had talked to Claire and I didn't want to say anything they could take the wrong way and get her in trouble. I didn't know what trouble they could make, but I've been leery of cops ever since I lived Down Neck where they had to be twice as tough as anybody else. This Flavin was no lily of the valley himself.

"That's right," he said. "Loomis walked out on her mother twenty years ago, leaving the woman with a girl of four to support. Never sent her any money, either. Did she tell you that, too?"

"More or less."

"Then, out of the blue, he sends the girl seventy-five dollars and asks her to meet him here in Newark. Surprising, isn't it?"

"He was sick. Arthritis deformis. He was going to have to give up his job."

"I know. I read the letter. That part of it is all right, but what I can't understand is why she came. He didn't even acknowledge her letter when she told him of the death of her mother two years ago. Why didn't she tell him to go to hell? But no, she practically gave up her job and came here all the way from Columbus, Ohio. I don't get it."

I didn't get it either, but I said, "He was her father and he was sick."

"According to her story, Malone, her mother brought her up to think of him as a bastard, and he was a bastard to leave his wife and kid destitute and never contribute a cent toward their support. Or don't you think so?"

"Sure, but what difference does it make?"

"Personally, I think a man like that deserves the public whipping post."

"He deserved something," I agreed.

"Love and affection? Care and sympathy?"

I thought of how Harry Loomis used to throw his

money around—setting up drinks for a gin-mill full of rummies, giving fifty-dollar wrist watches to whores, riding all over the country in cabs when he could have walked a block or two or taken a bus—playing the big shot just to show off, when what he spent in a single night would have kept his wife and Claire for a month, and it was a crummy thing to have done.

"No," I said.

"But that's exactly what the girl claims she came here prepared to give him—love and affection, care and sympathy."

He looked at me and his glance had "trap" written all over it. But the trap had been laid and I had already stepped into it. I had agreed with everything he said. I felt the skin crawl on the back of my neck—it felt like ants—but he didn't have me cornered. Yet.

"Women are different," I said, hoping to God I was going to be able to make some kind of sense. "They go for the crummiest guys. I agree with you—Loomis was a louse, but he was her father. He made a big pitch about being sick and she fell for it. Maybe it was a dumb thing to do but, damn it, I think a lot more of her because she did!"

It was an impassioned speech and I meant every word of it. Flavin smiled dryly and made another switch that caught me off-balance.

"This note of yours," he said, slapping it against the palm of his hand. "You thank him for a present. What was it?"

It was a trick and he had it down pat. He got you going at full speed in one direction, then switched and had you digging in your heels before you knew what was happening.

"There wasn't any present," I said, trying to get my wits together.

"No present? I don't understand. You mention a present in your note and Loomis spoke of it in his letter to his daughter. In fact, he said it was to be turned over to her in case anything happened to him, so he must have sent you something."

Oh damn, I thought tiredly, here we go again. So I told him how that big sailor, Jeff Buckley, had gotten drunk and lost the thing and I had thanked Loomis for a present just to keep Buckley out of trouble.

"And hell," I said, "I didn't think it was anything. His presents were always gags. Once it was a trick box of itching powder and another time it was a baby alligator that bit me."

Flavin listened without much expression, the way you'd listen to a sermon because you were in church and there wasn't anything else to listen to.

"How long have you known Buckley?" he asked.

"I don't know him at all. I never saw him before yesterday."

"You mean he was a stranger but you covered up his losing the present just to keep him out of trouble? You really go out of your way for strangers, don't you, Malone?"

"I just got finished telling you," I said, my voice getting louder, "I didn't give a damn about a present from Loomis. As far as I was concerned, it was probably a stink bomb, a lousy gag like all his other lousy gags."

He looked interested. "His gags made you sore?"

"The first time maybe, but not after that. When he sent me something, I knew what it would be— something to open under water."

"But this last one was different."

"You can't prove it by me. I never saw it."

He ignored me and went on as if thinking aloud. "It was earmarked for the daughter. He said so in his letter to her. He told her to look inside of it. He was expecting to get his hands on a lot of money at the end of this trip, so it probably had something to do with that. What do you think, Sergeant?"

"That sounds right, Lieutenant," said Gilman.

"So it wasn't a gag gift this time—it was something valuable, Right?"

"I think so too, Lieutenant."

"Very valuable, in fact. Loomis spoke of an investment that was going to set him up for life. It takes a pile of money to set up a man for life, even if he is in his fifties. No one aboard the boat knew anything about this investment, nor did anyone in the administration building of Trans-Ocean, so the investment must have been with somebody on the outside, somebody at this end of the trip, somebody here in Newark. I don't see any other way to figure it, do you, Sergeant?"

"That's the way I look at it too, Lieutenant."

"Loomis said he was fifty-three years old. How much would it take to set him up for life, Sergeant?"

Gilman knew the answer to that one, too. "The insurance companies say the average age is sixty-five. If Loomis was counting on supporting his daughter in Florida, he couldn't do it on much less than seventy-five a week."

"That would be about right, yeah, so it comes to thirty-eight hundred a year and for twelve years he would need exactly"—Flavin did a little quick mental arithmetic—"forty-five thousand six hundred dollars. But he spoke of buying a house too, Sergeant. You were in Florida last year. How much do houses run down there?"

"Well, the wife's cousin owns a place in Venice. That's on the Gulf of Mexico. It's a cement-block job, two bedrooms, one bath, and he gave ten thousand for it, but it's a kind of cheap house."

"Well, we'll say ten thousand, Sergeant—so roughly, to be fixed for life, Loomis would have needed fifty-five thousand dollars at a minimum. That is one hell of a lot of money."

"It ain't hay," Gilman agreed.

I wanted to laugh, only somehow I couldn't quite

raise it because both of them were looking at me as if I were no longer just plain Joe Malone. I was something else, something that they, as cops, found much more interesting. Their eyes were speculative and held that particular professional hostility with which cops regard those who break the law. They were also faintly ominous, like a pair of bird dogs on a point. Now I knew how a covey of quail felt.

"How about it, Malone?" Flavin asked softly.

"I just told you. I never got anything from Loomis." My throat felt as if it were full of fishbones. "Buckley got drunk and lost it before he got here. Ask him, he'll tell you."

"Buckley disappeared right after he had that argument with Loomis on the dock last night. Every cop in the city, county and state is looking for him."

"Look in the back rooms of the gin mills on Market Street. He was drunk all day yesterday, he was drunk last night, and he's probably drunk right now."

"We'll find him without your help, Malone, don't worry. We have a perfect description from the Trans-Ocean doctor, fingerprints and even a handful of snapshots that were taken and developed by the radio operator aboard the *Tranoco*. Sooner or later he'll have to come out from wherever he's hiding and a guy that big—six feet five, two hundred and forty pounds—he'll be spotted by the first beat cop he meets. Your friend hasn't a chance, Malone. He hasn't a prayer."

He was building up the pressure again, stepping up the pace, forcing me into one defensive denial after another, and it wasn't like in the ring where you could counter-punch.

"He isn't a friend," I said. "I saw him for the first time last night. He was asleep on the floor, drunk."

"How'd he get in? He had a key?"

"I don't know how he got in, but take a look at the lock on the door. You can open it by shoving a knife blade between the molding and the catch. I've done it myself when I left the keys in the car and didn't want to walk down and get them."

"You didn't know him at all?"

"No."

"So killing Loomis was all his own idea?"

"If he did, yes."

"So you're making him the patsy. He won't like that. He'll crucify you when we tell him. He'll lay out the whole deal like a Thanksgiving dinner."

"There wasn't any deal," I said, trying not to jump up and yell at him. "If Buckley killed Loomis, I don't know anything about it."

Gilman cleared his throat, very loud, very fake. Flavin turned and looked at him. "Yes, Sergeant?"

"This guy," Gilman pointed his chin at me, "I've been trying to place him. He used to be the bouncer for Abe Kinney's gambling joint on Frelinghuysen Avenue."

Flavin looked back at me and I said hotly, "So what? I was just the bouncer, I didn't run the joint, and hell, that was three years ago and I only worked there a month."

"And he was in the ring for a while, too," Gilman went on stolidly. "Fought under the name of Mick Malone. He hung around with that crowd at Curry's Gym on Market Street."

"Tell him the rest of it," I said angrily. "Tell him I worked there when they were short of sparring partners, which was ninety per cent of the time."

"You're getting excited again, Malone," said Flavin mildly.

"He's trying to make it sound as though I was one of the sharpshooters down there."

"You hung around with them," Gilman said.

"Not the angle boys, not the grifters. I never had anything to do with that stuff. Ask Curry if you don't believe me. And what difference does it make if I did bounce for Abe Kinney? I kept order and it was an honest job, not like the cops or politicians Abe paid off to let him stay open."

Gilman paid absolutely no attention except to wait till I got finished. "One of his pals," he told Flavin, "was Jimmy Corcoran. He's in the pen for auto theft."

"Well!" said Flavin thoughtfully, just as if he and Gilman hadn't talked this over before.

"And another pal of his," Gilman continued, "was Frankie Keogh, the punk that peddled numbers for the Zerkles. You remember Keogh. He was found on Mulberry Street, his head beaten in with a tire iron. This was in January. We got the word Keogh was holding out on collections, but nothing was ever proved. Corcoran, Keogh and Malone here all came from the same neighborhood Down Neck. They hung around together at Curry's."

"Nice friends you had, Malone," said Flavin dryly. "Does he have a record, Sergeant?"

It was an act. He knew damn well the kind of record I had, but it was all part of the pressure to break me down. And I had to sit there and take it.

"Well," said Gilman, "it ain't much as records go—disturbing the peace, drunk and disorderly, resisting arrest, reckless driving. Three convictions with fines. He never served time. But coming from Down Neck and running with the crowd he did, there's a lot of stuff we probably don't know. F'rinstance, he used to belong to the Atlas A. C. on West Market Street. That was the gang we cleaned out on a rape charge when twelve of them brought in two dames and got them drunk. But Malone wasn't in on that," he added with an air of giving me a break.

"Well," said Flavin, "well, well, well. Any comments, Malone?" He cocked his head and regarded me coldly.

My face felt frozen. "No comments," I said.

But inside I was raging to get at Gilman, just the

two of us in a room together with our bare fists. He was about five foot eleven, an inch shorter than I, but was thirty pounds heavier and had a pair of shoulders like a precast reinforced-cement lintel—but, man, in that moment I would have torn through him as if he were nothing more than stucco on chicken wire. The son of a bitch, he couldn't have made me sound worse if he had included me on that rape deal. Which wasn't rape at all, because I got the story later from Eaglebeak Murphy, a jerk the guys had kicked out of the A. C. when they brought the dames in. According to Eaglebeak, the dames were just passing through on their way to Atlantic City and agreed to take on the guys at a buck a head and then, with the evidence inside them, demanded a hundred bucks apiece or else. The guys had already paid up, some of them two and three times, the rabbits, and, liquored up, they got sore, took back their dough, kicked the dames out bare and threw their clothes after them. It might have been okay, but they got caught in the headlights of the prowl car, as they bent over pulling on their pants. Naturally they yelled rape to save getting themselves pulled in on a charge of drunk and disorderly and indecent exposure. But they were a pair of mudkickers and the cops and everybody else knew it and it was a bum rap for the guys and everybody knew that too, but there was nothing anybody could do about it. It was a rape neighborhood. Nobody in skirts, even if you were a grandmother, could walk down the street after dark with the gangs of vicious young punks roaming the streets, without being dragged in an alley, attacked and the hell beaten out of you afterward. Punks ten and fifteen years old.

But Gilman knew the gang at the A. C. never went in for that. They got drunk and had fights and, like he said, disturbed the peace, but they never beat up anybody but each other. I'm not trying to say they were just a bunch of Irish lads out for a bit of harmless fun because they weren't. Jimmy Corcoran went on from there to the pen, and Frankie Keogh got his brains beaten out by the Zerkles, and there were a few others I could name who had records worse than mine—Teddy McNamarra, Pudge O'Conner, Larry Cohan and Fingers Tracy, who was doing time for pocket-picking. Maybe I was the sissy, or maybe it was the old man's training, but I never stepped over the line except for D & D or resisting arrest the time a dumb rookie cop took a swing at me instead of just shoving me along into the wagon, the night I beat Sailor Tutchek at the Essex Arena and we were celebrating with a half keg of beer on the curb and making everybody who passed drink a glass.

I know, from the cops' point of view, we were a pain in the ass or worse, but Gilman didn't have to make me sound like a junior Dillinger. I wanted to rake out his guts and take Flavin for dessert, but this was serious and I held on till my knuckles turned white and ached from clenching my fists.

"No comment at all?" asked Flavin mockingly. "Come on, Malone, you can do better than that. You had plenty to say before."

"I said it all. No comment."

"Your record and background will make quite an impression on a jury."

"Let it."

I sat tight. It was all I could do.

He didn't like it. He grinned crookedly, one side of his mouth running up into his cheek. "You *want* to be booked?" he asked.

"You've got your mind made up," I said. "Take me in."

"He's tough, Lieutenant," said Gilman, looking me up and down like a butcher on a side of beef before he makes the cuts. "Real tough. You want I should soften him up, maybe?"

I gave Flavin the bare bones of a grin, all teeth.

"Let's go," I said. "Let him try. I've been wondering if I could take the big bastard."

"There are two of us," said Flavin expressionlessly.

"Then what're you waiting for?"

Gilman started from the door but Flavin waved him back with a vague flip of his hand. "What do you think all this is getting you, Malone?"

"Nothing. Absolutely nothing. I said your mind was made up, didn't I?"

Flavin shifted on the arm of the chair and re-crossed his legs. He took another cigarette from the pack in the breast pocket of his shirt and pointed it at me.

"Let me show you where you stand," he said, emphasizing each word with a jab of the cigarette. "Your record stinks. You're a tough mick from the Ironbound district of Newark—Down Neck—and half of your associates are in jail or dead. You happen to be in the clear at the moment and in business for yourself—a fringe business, if you don't mind my saying so—I know all about it, the second-hand and damaged crap you sell—but put yourself in on a jury and think it over, you and Jeff Buckley standing trial for a murder charge."

"Not me," I said. "I didn't murder anybody."

"Maybe you don't realize what you're up against. You had a deal with Harry Loomis, which was supposed to net him between fifty and sixty thousand dollars. He called it an investment, but I'm not going to ask any questions. Okay. The deal goes through and you're holding his end of it, a big hunk of dough. Jeff Buckley was in on it some way or another because he made the delivery to you. Now"—he inched himself forward on the arm of the chair and pointed the cigarette at me like a finger—"here you are holding, say, sixty thousand dollars belonging to Loomis, but with Loomis out of the way, you and Buckley can split that amount. As I said before, that's a hell of a lot of money, particularly to a guy like you. So what happens? You think, the hell with Loomis, sixty thousand bucks, that's mine, I worked for it, I'm the one who has to do the dirty work, I have to peddle this stuff, I take all the risks and Loomis gets the gravy, nuts to him!"

It must have been just the sheer craziness of it that stiffened me up, because I leaned toward him and stuck out my chin. "What dirty work?" I demanded. "And what gravy?"

Flavin pulled his hand down the side of his jaw and gave me such a smug, knowing grin that if he hadn't been a cop and there was nothing I could do about it, I'd have given him a face full of knuckles he couldn't have digested for ten generations, and it was all I could do to hold myself in while he waved that cigarette at me like a teacher lecturing a moron.

"We cops aren't as dumb as you think, Malone," he said, pityingly. "We've been doing a little checking up on this investment angle of Loomis. *And* on Loomis himself. We know, for instance, you weren't with him the last time he touched Newark, four months ago. He ranged high, wide and handsome for almost a week and spent nearly a thousand bucks. It's just not me talking to you, Malone"—he tapped himself on the chest with the fingers of both hands, leaning even closer—"I'm only one cop and Sergeant Gilman here is only another. There are hundreds of us, thousands— city, county and state, and national, if it comes to that. We're an organization, we're *big*, and a pair of grifters like you and Loomis are peanuts. Get *that* through you head, once and for all. Peanuts! All I have to do is snap my fingers and a million wheels go into motion, adding, subtracting, dividing, and all coming out with the sum total of a punk named Joe Malone. We have your fingerprints from the time you were in the Navy, we have every report card on you from the first grade on up, we know your father's ancestors and damn near every bitch you ever laid. Who the hell do you think you are? I know more about you right this minute than you know about yourself. You don't think so? Okay. Just let me tell you something that might shake you up. On the Labor Day weekend of Nineteen Fifty-five you took a girl named Ellen Ogilvy to Lake Hopatcong. You started at nine in the morning with a picnic lunch in a shoebox. You went to the public beach at Buter's Island and took a table near the litter pier they have. It's now around eleven-thirty. You went into the bathhouse and changed into your bathing suits. You're quite a diver and you gave an exhibition for about fifteen minutes, particularly with the jack-knife because it was a low board. Do you want me to go on?"

"I know the rest of it," I said, "but you don't have it exactly right. It wasn't the Labor Day weekend, it was just Labor Day, and on Tuesday Ellen Ogilvy's dumb brother went to the precinct station yelling I'd ruined his sister but the desk sergeant talked him out of it because and you could hardly walk down the street without meeting a guy who hadn't given it to her at some time or other, and even that part of it's cockeyed. She wasn't with me, she was with Dinny Malone from Beech Street. I was with a girl named Janice Noonan and we didn't go to Lake Hopatcong, we went to Asbury Park."

It did me good to be able to tell him that, believe me. Gilman flushed but Flavin said indifferently, "All Malones are alike, it seems. Just for the record, however, where were you last night between eleven and twelve?"

"Right here with Miss Loomis, waiting for her father," I said.

"And the two of you were at the gate of Trans-Ocean at one o'clock, an hour after Loomis was killed only two hundred feet down the road."

"What's that supposed to mean?"

"You tell me."

A picture of that brightly lighted gate area came up in my mind, that island of brilliance in an ocean of night, four big floodlights on flanking pylons. I looked at Flavin.

"Something's screwy," I said.

I'll give Flavin this much—he didn't have a one-track mind. He must have seen I had something because his eyes sharpened and he demanded alertly, "What are you talking about?"

"Have you ever been at Trans-Ocean at night?"

He shook his head. "So?"

"The gate is floodlighted and you can read a newspaper two hundred feet up the road. Pulling a killing there would like staging it at the corner of Broad and Market."

Flavin looked quickly at Gilman, who nodded, frowning. "He's right about that. You can see the lights the minute you turn off from the airport."

Flavin turned back to me. "What's the point?" he demanded.

"Well" I said, fumbling, "everybody takes it for granted Loomis climbed the fence at the gate because the watchman was making the rounds and he didn't feel like waiting for him to come back. That doesn't make sense unless he had a cab waiting, and there was a phone in the watchman's shack and he could have called a cab, but if there was a cab he wouldn't have been killed out there. I mean, he would have climbed the fence, gotten in the cab and ridden off. If he were stopped, the hack would have been involved, too, and you'd have had a report on a missing cab. Unless," I added lamely, "the hack driver was mixed up in it, too."

Flavin was very still and the cigarette he had used as an accusing finger was motionless in his hand. "Keep going," he said.

"Well," I floundered, feeling my way along, "I don't think he climbed the fence at the gate. I think he climbed it some place else, in the dark, where he couldn't be seen. I think he wanted to get out without anybody knowing."

"Why?"

"I don't know, but I just can't see him climbing the fence by the gate in the middle of all those lights unless he had a cab waiting, and there's no reason for him climbing it any place else unless he was sneaking out."

"Why should he sneak out?" Flavin asked intently. "What was he afraid of?"

"I don't know."

"Did you threaten him over the phone when he called you, Malone? The watchman claims Loomis kept asking you not to be sore at him. Why was he afraid of you?"

We were right back where we started and I felt as if I were knee-deep in quicksand and trying to sprint away from a savage dog snapping at my legs.

"I didn't threaten him," I said, clenching my teeth; the pressure was on again. "And he wasn't afraid of me."

"But he was begging you not to be sore at him."

"We've been all over this before."

"Sure, but I'd like to know what you said to scare Loomis into climbing the fence in the dark."

"I didn't say anything."

"But you just got finished making a very nice description of him sneaking out of the Trans-Ocean property, and you couldn't have made that kind of sense without knowing something about it. What did Loomis send you that was worth between fifty-five and sixty thousand dollars? Just his share. What was this investment? What were you peddling for him?"

"Nothing. And I don't know anything about his investments."

"And you don't know the first port the *Tranoco* hit in California was San Diego and San Diego is less than fifty miles north of the Mexican border?"

"Why should I know that? I didn't even know his boat was named *Tranoco* till last night."

"And you don't know that Mexico is one of the biggest producers of heroin in the world and that you can get a hundred thousand dollars' worth of heroin in a package no bigger than a birthday cake—except in this case it would be a deathday cake. Heroin is a drug."

"I know what it is," I said angrily, without thinking.

"Sure you know what it is," Flavin purred. "Some of your friends probably used it. It's a narcotic, Malone, a morphine derivative, and when you start fooling around with that stuff, you have the federal government on your neck."

I thought sickly, so that's what Loomis was playing with, that was his "investment." He was one of the death merchants.

"I swear to God, Flavin," I said violently, "I'd kill any s.o.b. I caught pushing that stuff!"

"Loomis, for instance, Malone?"

I knew I'd said too much but I couldn't help it and wouldn't have taken a word of it back. You can't stop a bartender from selling a rummy a drink, but a dope pusher was less than the scum on a septic tank. I *would* kill the bastard if I caught him.

"Yes," I said belligerently, knowing I was sticking my neck out, "Loomis, for instance, or anybody else. And if I caught a pervert torturing babies, like that crud in Philadelphia, I'd beat the louse till the marrow came out of his bones like toothpaste. And if you want to make anything out of it, you cold-hearted mother-lover, go right ahead!"

He didn't even blink. "Quite a speech," he said. "Right, Sergeant?"

"Yeah," said Gilman, eyeing me narrowly.

Flavin rose and shrugged his jacket more snugly around his shoulders. "This has been very interesting,

Malone, and you don't have a thing to worry about—till we catch up with Jeff Buckley. And it would be just too bad if we found him dead, wouldn't it? Let's go, Sergeant."

They walked out and I stood there for a long time staring at the closed door, hardly able to believe it was over, if only for the time being. I wiped my hand across my face, held it up and looked at it. My fingers were shaking and wet.

Four

The door opened and Flavin looked in. "We've had Miss Loomis' phone blocked off at the hotel switchboard all day," he said, "but you can call her now. I'll leave word." He closed the door in my face as I made a plunging step toward him.

I walked stiffly to the window and stood there, looking down, till I saw him and Gilman slide into the police car and drive away. I was numb and at the same time wanted to smash my fist into something that would break. I went into the kitchen and poured myself a heavy drink of applejack. It went down like water, without taste, flavor or impact. That Flavin was the coldest man I'd ever met. He dredged you out, scraped you raw and bloody, hoed you hollow. He left you in a futile fury, swinging at cobwebs that clung to your face in wispy nothingness. He built up the pressure till you couldn't contain it, then swung around and built it up from another direction, never giving you leverage against him, always leaving you with the earth falling away from under your feet, and in the end you were a defensive knot with your fists gripped so tight that the knuckles were white and pointed and your muscles ached from holding a tight guard and trying to roll with his punches.

Logically, the case he had against me wouldn't have stood up in traffic court on a parking ticket, but you couldn't think logically when he got done with you. He left you fighting the *ifs* and *buts* and *maybes* and gnawing the worry to the quick. He gave you the rope with the knot already tied and showed you the beam over which you could throw it and even provided the basket to carry out the body. He wasn't a man—he was doom, spelled D-O-O-M. The man with the scythe, the last breath you can't catch, the grave and the cremation, the final trap.

I was just in the mood when the doorbell sounded. It wasn't the apartment house lobby because that one was a buzzer. It was my own personal hall doorbell that shrilled like a cicada. I swung out of the kitchen, strode across the living room and opened the door. He came in fast with a short-barreled gun against my belly, my buck-toothed friend of last night, the one who had potted me over the ear with a blackjack. His lips were drawn back, showing every thrusting denture, and he hit me with the gun as if it were a knife.

"Okayokayokay," he panted, as if he had run up the three flights of stairs the moment Flavin and Gilman drove away. "Just take it easy and nobody gets hurt." He kicked the door shut with a backward flip of his foot, "We're going places, you and me."

I had backed up three paces out of sheer surprise and the weight of him against me, but what he didn't know was I was boiling over and his shove was the last straw and his gun in my belly didn't mean any more than a teething ring. I slapped it aside with my left hand and, pivoting, brought up a right from the hip that caught him flush on the point of his surprised jaw. His head snapped back, his feet flew up, and he slammed against the door with a crash that would have brought joy to the hearts of the carpenters' union. He seemed to be pasted there against the panels and I hit him three more times with a left and a right and a left, all to the jaw, before he slid down and collapsed bonelessly on the rug.

I bent over and snatched up the gun that had skidded out of his hand against the baseboard. I took him by the collar, dragged him across the room and heaved him into the sofa. His head bounced against the arm with a thunk, the cushion springs threw him up and he subsided with one arm dangling to the floor, flat on his back, jaw slack, eyes rolled up, the picture of a perfect kayo.

I stood over him, my chest heaving. If he had moved

as much as an eyelid, I swear to God, I'd have gun-whipped him raw. I hovered, waiting for him to move, but he was out cold. I was actually quivering with the desire to smash something. I slapped him back and forth across the face, twisted his ears, jammed up his nostrils with the heel of my hand, tried every way I knew to make him move, but he was really in cold storage.

I must have been out of my mind. There's no other explanation for it. I went out to the kitchen, got a tray of ice cubes and held them against his forehead, cheeks and neck, to bring him around just so I could smack him again. I couldn't hit him while he was unconscious. He had to be awake so he could feel it. I wanted him on his feet, I wanted him to put up his hands so I could go through his guard and feel the satisfaction of slamming in a left and a right and a left and a right to his chin. I wanted to hit him till his jaw broke and it felt like swinging into a bag of marbles. I was crazy. I know it. Panting, I ran out to the kitchen again, slamming through the cupboards, looking for the bottle of ammonia. If I could just get that bottle of ammonia, I could hold it under his nose and bring him around, stand him on his feet and wade into him with both hands. There was no ammonia. I'd never had any in the first place. It was Kubec, my next door neighbor, who'd held the bottle of ammonia to my nose last night. I didn't have any. Insanely, I thought of running next door to Kubec's and borrowing his bottle of ammonia, but he'd ask questions and I'd have to get rid of him.

I ran back to the living room, breathing heavily. My boy was still dead to the world. I took him by the ears, lifted him up and threw him down. There was no more life in him than a side of beef. For a minute I thought I'd killed him, and grabbed for his wrist, but his pulse was slow and steady. I swore and threw his hand back in his face. I still had his gun in my hand. It was a .38, one of those short-barreled jobs they call a Bankers Special. I could empty it into him and nobody'd give a damn. I could blow his guts into the sofa springs. But I didn't want it that way. I wanted him to feel it and I didn't want to give it to him with a gun. It was something I had to do with my bare hands. And this is what Flavin had done to me.

He lay on his back, mouth open, his buck teeth bunched under his upper lip like a—like a rabbit!

A rabbit.

Maybe that's what brought me back to sanity before I killed him, and I would have killed him if he had stirred. A rabbit. Those buck teeth. My memory stirred, churning. A rabbit and buck teeth. No wonder I thought he looked familiar. He damn well was familiar. I knew the bastard. He was Bunny Riordan, a kid who used to live one street over from me Down Neck. We were both fourteen or fifteen, but he had worn glasses in those days. Four-eyes, we called him, but when he went into a fight he had bent strap-iron across his knuckles and cleats in his shoes. He came at you screaming and sobbing and flailing away like a windmill and the guys thought he was nuts and left him alone. Later on he moved out of the neighborhood, and still later I heard he was working for the Zerkles, though a lot of guys, who didn't, were supposed to be working for the Zerkles or Longy Zwillman, the Bergen Street boss of Jersey.

But this was Bunny Riordan, all right, minus his glasses and sixty pounds heavier. You couldn't miss those buck teeth, which gave him his nickname. Bunny Riordan. I looked dazedly at the gun in my hand, his gun. It gives you a funny feeling to meet a kid from the old neighborhood and find he's gone one way and you've gone another, and he's actually the guy who raided your apartment and belted you over the ear with a blackjack and stuck a gun in your belly.

My hands had begun to shake again—the reaction,

I suppose—and I sat down in the lounge chair and lit a cigarette. Bunny Riordan was really out for the long count. It was five minutes before he stirred and opened his narrow-set, squinty eyes. He didn't come out of it dazed and slack-jawed, but fully aware of where he was and figuring how to get out of it. He had probably been conscious for a few minutes but had lain there with his eyes closed till he had things straight. He had always been that way, a shrewd onion, even as a kid. He sat up slowly, watching the gun.

"Hi, Bunny," I said grimly. "How are things with you these days?"

His eyes spread but quickly thinned and searched my face. I'd bet he hadn't heard that nickname for years. "What's the gag?"

"Don't you remember me? We went to high school together. We were buddies, except I had to kick your tail once in a while when you got snotty."

"Oh," he said nastily, "so you're that Malone. The dumb mick from Down Neck."

"Nice of you to drop in, Bunny. What's on your mind?"

"Just passing through," he said, still watching the gun.

"It was quite a surprise, but now that you're here, I hope you'll stay a while. It's been fifteen years since the last time I booted your tail. I might even do it again, just for old times' sake."

"A clown," he said disgustedly. "A lousy comedian."

"And it was nice seeing you last night, too, Bunny. It was good to see a buddy again."

"Last night," he said, not quite yawning, "I was in Hackensack with a party of friends."

"You must be mistaken, Bunny. You were right here. I walked in and you were so glad to see me that you clouted me over the ear with a blackjack. Or was it a length of rubber hose stuffed with sand? You were always a one for carrying things like that around with you. Remember the Bull Durham bag on a string, full of BB's, you used to keep in your back pocket? Many a guy got slapped in the snoot with that. And the brass knuckles you made out of one-inch strap iron, and how you used to make snowballs, dip them in water and freeze them, and the time you nailed three feet of barbed wire to a handle and went for Pudge Ryan till his hands and arms and chest and back looked like a busted blood bank? Those were the days, weren't they, Bunny? You were full of surprises and the guys never knew what you'd spring on them next. The broken glass in the foot of an old stocking. You almost got me with that one but I ducked and beat the living hell out of you. Kids sure have fun, don't they?"

"Too bad I missed. But now what, comedian? Going to turn me over to the cops?"

"Maybe. They'd be glad to see you, too."

"Go ahead, but it won't get you anything. I drop in to see an old friend on his invitation and he pulls a gun on me and says he's going to turn me in because he's in dutch himself and needs a patsy to make an impression on the cops. Go ahead, call headquarters. There's the phone."

"Shrewd," I said admiringly, "real shrewd, but you were always a guy to figure the angles, always one step ahead of the rest of us dumb clunks. So maybe I won't call the cops. It's more comfortable here anyway."

"You won't use the gun, Malone. You've always been too chicken."

"You mean because I never used the knucks, a zip gun or a knife, or any of those gadgets you invented? Maybe you're right, but there never was a day I couldn't take you with my bare hands. Maybe I'll keep you around and beat you up from time to time, just for kicks."

He measured me silently, thinking it over. He was as big as I, and heavier, but I knew he couldn't put up a fight because he had always depended on gadgets.

"Now, Bunny," I said, "let's get down to business. What were you doing here last night? We'll start there."

"I was in Hackensack."

"I wish I had a Bible so you could swear to it, but I don't think I'd be impressed. What were you looking for? That thing Harry Loomis is supposed to have sent me?"

It was a wild guess but his eyes flickered for a second before he made them blank. "Who's Loomis?" he asked.

"A guy they found dead this morning. He was beaten over the head with something hard and heavy like, for instance, that tire iron you laid open Red Flannery's head with the time you got him after school behind the fence near Minotti's grocery store. Come to think of it, the cops might not believe that yarn about your just dropping in on an old friend. They might even get to thinking you were a friend of Harry Loomis, too. You were always a little rough on your friends, even in the old days, Bunny. They might be interested in that, too, and how you escaped reform school by the skin of your teeth the time you threw a pair of pliers at Mr. Knowles in history class."

"Who's Loomis?" he repeated without expression.

"What is this thing Harry is supposed to have sent me? I never got it. In some ways Harry wasn't very bright. A smart guy wouldn't have used a rummy for a messenger boy. The clunk got soused and lost it. But I'd like to clear up the mystery. What was the thing?"

Something lurked behind his squinty eyes but nothing showed except a slight narrowing of the eyelids, and his buck teeth made him look like a stuffed rabbit.

"I don't know Loomis," he said woodenly, "so how do I know what he sent you?"

"No? You made an awful mess out of my

apartment last night. What were you looking for, Bunny? I'm not kidding. I want to know."

He looked faintly amused and contemptuous. "Go to hell," he said.

I leaned suddenly forward and he threw up his arms to protect his face, but I rapped him on the kneecap with the flat off the gun. He sucked in his breath from the pain but made no other sound. His eyes were clotted with hate.

"You're going to tell me if I have to beat you up from now on," I said. "You know me, Bunny. I don't kid around when it comes to something like this. I'm not squeamish with my hands, and you know that, too. I've smacked you often enough. Now start talking."

"I don't know anything about it," he said in a stony voice.

In a way, he had me. Even as a kid he'd never let out a whimper even when he was getting the hell kicked out of him. The only time he bawled was when he was crazy mad.

That rap on the kneecap must have been excruciating, but he'd only sucked in his breath. In that way he was tougher than the kids who used to beat him up. Stubborn tough, all knotted up inside.

"All right," I said. "We'll go on to something else for the moment. When you walked in and shoved your gun in my belly, you said we were going places. What places?"

"No place. I was going to give it to you right here."

"Give me what?"

"In that last fight we had, you broke my nose. I never forget. I saw your name in the phone book and decided now was the time to return the favor."

"You're a liar. You tore my place apart last night looking for something and today you came back with a gun. Where were you supposed to take me, hotshot?"

"I told you."

"If I keep hammering on your kneecap I might bust

it. How'd you like to walk with a limp for the rest of your life?"

His face looked like old mutton fat but he merely compressed his lips and sat there, hating me. "Go ahead," he said.

He swung at me and he made a grab for the gun, but I was expecting it and let him have it alongside the face, opening a cut on his cheekbone. The blood trickled down his face but he wouldn't lift his hand to check it.

"I won't forget that one either, Malone," he said.

"That's only the beginning," I said savagely. "We've got all night. There'll be a lot of other things you won't forget, too, and you won't be in any condition to do anything about it, not for a long time to come."

"But there'll still be a time."

"There's another way, too. You're a smart boy but not smart enough to be in on this alone. You're taking orders from somebody. According to Lieutenant Flavin, a tough cop from homicide, Harry Loomis had his hands on something like sixty thousand dollars. That's important money, too big for a gun punk like you. So you're working for somebody and I have an idea he's a tougher man than you and me put together. So this is what I think I'll do. I'll turn you over to Flavin. It'll be no job for him to trace back and find out who your boss is. You're right about one thing. I'm chicken. I might put you in the hospital, but I wouldn't finish you off. However, your boss might not be so finicky if he thinks you might lead the cops to him, and being in jail won't help you a bit. Guys have been knocked off in a cell before this. Think about it for a minute, Riordan. What kind of guy is your boss? Will he say, 'Dear me, this is most distressing,' or will he send somebody down to the jailhouse and slip a knife into you? Or maybe he'll get you out on bail, and tomorrow they'll find you in the mud out in the

Secaucus swamp. If they find you at all, that is. Go on, think about your boss. How happy will he be with you in the hands of a smart, hard-boiled cop like Flavin. You might not have very long to live, Bunny."

It was my own fault. I thought I had him cold. I had the gun but even if I didn't, he wouldn't have stood a chance against me. I could hit harder and faster and slap him silly before he could get his hands up. That was me, Joe Malone, with everything under control. I had him where I wanted him and there wasn't a thing he could do about it. No, sir.

Except I was so full of myself I forgot for a moment he was a smart onion and not for an instant had he stopped figuring and scheming and laying a way out for himself. Also, I had hit the nail on the head with that business about his boss and he had to do something fast. He did. Bit by bit he had inched his feet under the cocktail table in front of the sofa and suddenly he threw up his legs and the heavy maple table slammed straight in my face. The edge of it caught me on the bridge of the nose and the room disappeared for a minute in swirls of flashing lights. The tears streamed out of my eyes from the abrupt, crashing pain, blinding me further.

He didn't hang around and take the chance of snatching the gun from me. He was up from the sofa and out of the room while I was still groggily fighting to get the table out of my lap. The door slammed before I could stumble to my feet, my eyes watering so badly it was like trying to peer through Niagara Falls. He was gone, except for the sound of his skittering feet on the stairs, by the time I got to the door and could see again. That was one thing he'd always been better at than anybody else—he could run. He could run like a charged greyhound and there hadn't been a kid in the neighborhood fast enough to catch him. I swore and sprinted down the stairs and out to the sidewalk, but there was nothing to be seen of him, and I swore again, remembering that he wouldn't be so dumb as to use the front entrance—he'd go out the back and lose me in the maze of alleys and backyard fences.

I must have been quite a sight, glaring wildly up and down the street, still clutching the gun, swearing. Bivens stood on the corner, his jaw sagging, and the girl beside him had her hand to her mouth, her eyes two startled O's of astonishment and fright.

I shoved the gun into my back pocket, literally grinding my teeth. I'd been suckered by a trick so old I'd seen it a hundred times in the movies. I think I was madder at myself than at Riordan. As I swung back toward the front door, the girl with Bivens called my name and at the sound of her voice I felt as if I had been pierced by a bolt of quivering blue-hot lightning, just like that. It was a voice I'd never forget—husky, intimate, promising, but beneath it was a heart as chilly as a bank statement. I'd carried a torch for her since we were kids down in the Ironbound and eight months ago she'd given me the brushoff for Jack Garrity, a minor big shot in City Hall. She was on the make and I was too smalltime for her.

Janice Noonan, her curly blue-black hair cropped with a suggestion of abandon, like an Italian actress, came walking quickly toward me, carrying a newspaper, an expensive alligator bag swinging from a strap over her shoulder. Blue eyes and that wonderful creamy complexion. In that crummy neighborhood, on that sidewalk littered with blown newspapers, bits of refuse the dogs had dragged from the garbage cans and the runny-nosed kids playing in the gutter, she was as vivid and breathtaking as a wingless angel, dark and tormenting.

"You? It's you?" I said stupidly.

There were still traces of apprehension in the oval of her fabulous face. "For Heaven's sake, Joe," she cried, "what happened?"

"A guy tried to hold me up and I lost him. He

kicked a table in my face and beat it while I was falling all over myself."

"Good Lord! But—why—I mean, he held you up?"

"He wanted something I didn't have," I growled. "But come to think of it, what're you doing here? Slumming?"

She looked reproachfully at me. "Is that your only greeting, Joe?"

"All right—how are you? But what are you doing here?"

"I thought you were in trouble, Joe," she said gravely, "I read in the paper the police were looking for you." She showed me the newspaper. "It said they wanted you for questioning about that man who was killed last night at Port Newark."

"What were you going to do, hold my hand?" I was in a turmoil at the sight of her, all the old emotions boiling up, but I was still bitter, even after all these months.

"I wanted to help if I could, Joe," she said quietly, "You're an old friend and I don't forget old friends, even though we did fight like Kilkenny. I know some influential people in town, you know, and I hated the thought of your being hunted by the police when I might be able to help."

"I'm not hunted anymore," I said roughly. "They found me."

"And—everything is all right?"

"I'm not in jail, am I?"

"All right, Joe. I'll go if you feel like that. But I'm glad you're not in trouble."

Only yesterday I was aching to see her or just talk to her on the phone and, oh, all the bad nights when the darkness crouched over the bed, pressing me down with the shards and splinters of memory. I wanted to let her go—it would be better all around—but she had me and the stifling need I had for her was almost as strong as ever.

"Hell," I said, "you don't have to rush right off, unless you're in a hurry."

"Not that much of a hurry, Joe."

"All right, then. Let's go down to the gin mill and have a drink, if you don't mind being seen in public with a truck driver. That's what I am. I drive a truck for a living these days."

I wasn't being pitiful or sorry for myself. I wanted to punish her a little.

She laughed. "Don't let these clothes fool you. I'm not Miss Rich Bitch. And don't forget, my father was a truck driver for the Hudson and Essex Home Laundry."

"The gin mill's just around the corner. It's a real high class joint. The guys won't spit on the floor or say son of a bitch with ladies present."

"I'm not afraid to go to your apartment for a cocktail, Joe," her eyes were laughing at me. "It wouldn't be the first time."

"Let's not bring that up," I said shortly. "It's dead and buried. Anyway, the place looks like a wrestling match at a rummage sale."

I took her around the corner to the Shamrock Bar, which wasn't anywhere as rough as I'd let on. In fact, it was a kind of family place where the neighbors took their wives at night sometimes for a glass of beer, a look at TV or a game of shuffleboard. The bartender was a husband and a father and was always bragging about his wife's cooking, his kid who played football in high it school or the big beefsteak tomatoes he grew in his back yard. There were booths at the side with Formica tops that looked like green cloth. The bartender came over for a closer look at Janice and wiped the table with a towel.

"The lady'll have a cocktail," I said. "If you don't know how to make cocktails, we'll have to take our trade to the Stork Club."

Janice smiled at him. "I'll have a boilermaker," she

said. "Rye with a beer chaser. I still like an honest drink, Joe."

"Make mine the same," I said, "and don't forget a bowl of pig's knuckles and popcorn. We're just a couple of shanty Irish out on a spree. Five minutes from now we'll be fighting on the floor and trying to gouge each other's eyes out. You know us Irish."

Janice crinkled her eyes at the bartender. "Is he always like this?" she asked.

"Naw," he told her. "Sometimes he washes his face."

When he left to build the drinks, she smiled intimately at me as if we really were old friends. "It is nice seeing you again," she said. "That is, it would be if you wiped that tough Down Neck scowl off your face."

"It grew this way," I said, still taking a slap at her. "I was disappointed in love."

"Joe, please don't."

She looked suddenly saddened, but not overdoing it and I felt like a jerk.

"All right," I said. "I'll stop. I guess I'm still a little sore because you gave me the brushoff for Garrity, the City Hall big shot."

"I didn't give you the brushoff," she said indignantly. "I went out with him only because he was getting me a job singing in the Flamingo Club. You brushed *me* off, if you remember. You called me every name in the book, said I was on the make and could go to hell. Hardly the tender sentiments a girl likes to hear."

"All right. I've got a bad temper, but let's forget it. The last time I heard, you were in South America."

"That was months ago, just a little vacation."

"Still singing at the Flamingo Club?"

"Oh, dear me, no. I've come up in the world, I'll have you know. I'm the star at the opening of the new and veddy, veddy snazzy Esplanade House tonight. My dear, it's the most. A tourist trap," she added out of the side of her mouth. "Steak sandwiches at six bucks a throw. And I'm not a singer any more, Joe. I'm a chanteuse. That means they turn down the lights and I lean against the piano, twist a piece of red nylon in my hands and sing in a low, sexy voice as if I am bored to death but need only the right man to snap me out of it."

"You can sing," I grinned, "and you don't have pretend to be sexy."

"Oh, shut up, you big lout. I'm not sexy. I'm just a clean-living girl with healthy appetites. And you're not addressing Janice Noonan, dear. I'm Felice Daudet—and I know five whole songs in French, half a one in Spanish, and three in what might pass for Italian if you happened to be Swedish. But honestly, Joe," she said seriously, "I am glad you're not in trouble with the police. What was it all about? The newspaper sounded so ominous."

"Just a guy I knew casually, that's all. But you know the cops. They question everybody in sight when there's a killing. It makes a big show and looks good to the reporters. I didn't murder anybody."

"I never thought you did, Joe, but—I really did want to help, if I could. I know both Mayor Hadley and District Attorney Leonard well enough to ask them the score."

"It won't come to that. I'm in the clear."

"You're sure?"

"Positive."

"Well, I'm not. I know you, Joe Malone. You're a pig-headed Irishman and sometimes too independent for your own good. When you turn stubborn, you'd rather break your neck before you'll let anybody help you."

"Okay," I said, "help me, then. Lend me your iron lung."

"I'm serious, Joe. That newspaper story scared me.

I think I'll ask around a little, just so I can be sure."

"Oh for God's sake," I said uneasily. "If I were in a jam on the killing, I wouldn't be walking around loose, would I?"

"I don't know. I want to find out." She gave me a straight, level glance, not sexy but earnest and concerned. "Strangely enough, I still do feel a certain affection for you, even if I am a tramp, a bitch and on the make and all those other things you told me. And believe it or not, I treasure old friends. Why"—she gave a small, inquiet laugh—"I may need an old friend myself some day."

She quickly reached out and rapped three times on the side of the table. Knocking on wood. She had always been just a little superstitious. And there was something in that defenseless, little-girl gesture that caught at me more sharply than the sight of her fullness, the sound of her voice or the feel of her closeness. She was still Janice Noonan, my first girl, who had stuck in my mind and heart like a burr.

But as I'd told her, it was dead and buried and I wanted it to stay that way. For my own good.

To keep the conversation from getting too personal, I said, "Yeah, there's nothing like old friends. There's one thing you can always depend on them for, to put the bite on you for a fin or a sawbuck."

"Don't talk like that, Joe. It's cynical."

"Do you remember Bunny Riordan?" I asked. "A crud with buck teeth."

Her forehead wrinkled. "I think so. Didn't he throw a knife at Mr. Knowles in history class that time?"

"A pair of pliers."

"I remember him now. I was scared to death of him. He used to carry a horrible little knife he made from a hacksaw blade, sawteeth on one side and a razor edge on the other."

"He was always making things like that. A nice

guy, an old friend from the old neighborhood. Well, he's the guy who just tried to hold me up."

"Good Lord! Why?"

"Somebody sent him after a package I didn't get from Harry Loomis. Flavin—he's a homicide dick—has the idea it was heroin smuggled in from Mexico. That's why the pressure's on."

"Dope! Ugh!" she shivered. "The drummer at the Flamingo smoked reefers. He gave me the creeps. You—weren't mixed up with Loomis in that, were you, Joe?"

"No, and I hope Loomis wasn't either. I used to like the guy. But if he was, I didn't know anything about it. Anyway, I never got the package."

"I knew you wouldn't get mixed up with dope, Joe," she said. I couldn't understand why she was so relieved. We weren't really anything to each other now, hardly even old friends. Then she worried again. "Could he have been playing you for a sucker, Joe—using your place for a drop? They have to keep changing their drops, you know."

"If it were that, he'd have said, 'Hold this package for me, Joe,' or something like that, but he called it a present."

I didn't mention that the "present" was supposed to go to Claire if something happened to Harry, and he'd hardly have sent her sixty thousand dollars' worth of heroin. She wouldn't know what to do with it. Unless that letter was a fake and she wasn't his daughter, after all. But she couldn't get away with that, not with Flavin having the Columbus cops put an immediate check on her, which would be routine in a killing.

"I have a feeling he was using you for a sucker in some way, Joe," Janice said in a troubled voice. "What was so valuable about the package? Why did Bunny Riordan try to hold you up for it?"

"The package was lost, so I wouldn't know."

"Don't go against the police, Joe," she pleaded. "I've seen too much of it. You know what happened to Timmy."

I said, "Yeah." Timmy was her brother. He was doing time for holding up a gas station. "But if the package turned up now, Flavin would never believe me. Anyway, I'm nosey, Janice. Now I want to know what's in it."

"Don't fool with it, Joe! Don't have anything to do with it. Throw it in the garbage. Don't even open it. Then you won't have to pretend you don't know anything about it. They'll find out, they'll trip you up."

"Well," I said, not wanting to talk about it, "maybe you're right."

"I'm right, Joe. Believe me. They're shrewder than you think. Timmy thought he was smart, you could never talk to him, now look where he is."

"All right. I'm convinced. Let's forget it."

"You're angry with me?"

"No, I'm just tired of the whole thing. I'm tired of tough cops and guys pointing guns at me. I want to forget it. I don't want to think about anything except the day's work ahead of me tomorrow."

She smiled uncertainly and put a hesitant hand on my arm. It was the first time I'd seen her unsure of herself. "I hate to think of people I know turning out like Timmy. It's so—wasteful. But let's forget it. I don't want to brood about it either. But listen," she ran on with a brittle show of gaiety, "why don't you come to the opening of the Esplanade tonight?"

"Oh sure," I said. "Steak sandwiches at six bucks a throw. A hamburger and a glass of beer, that's my speed these days, honey. Anyway, I have a date," I lied.

"Bring her. It's open house tonight, everything free. By invitation only, but I have an extra ticket."

She took the ticket from her handbag. It was engraved on a thin piece of yellowish metal in an ornate plastic border like an old-fashioned picture frame. She ran her fingertips over the shining metal.

"Real gold," she said reverently. "Somebody told me the tickets alone cost fifty dollars apiece."

"And I'll bet you have to turn them in at the door."

"No, they're souvenirs. You can keep them."

"Then they'll make it back in steak sandwiches. And how much is a glass of water? Two bucks?"

"If you come, I'll reserve a table for you. I like the idea of having someone there who knew me when, someone who wouldn't sit and watch and not give a damn if I flopped. Come—just for luck."

So I was going to be her rabbit's foot for the evening, her lucky horseshoe, her four-leaf clover. She might look like a beautiful, sophisticated, gorgeous-type piece, but at bottom she was superstitious Irish, crouched over a peat fire, mumbling spells to ward off the evil eye at the trembling minute of midnight. I turned the "ticket" in my hand. What the hell. Why turn down a chance to free-load? And I could use an evening out.

"Okay," I said. "I'll be your luck. You can't miss, honey. You've got what the Esplanade needs. You even look expensive. But what'll I do with this damn ticket? Hang it piously around my neck like a scapular?"

"Don't talk like that," she said in horror. "It's bad luck to make fun of the Church."

"Slip of the tongue. I'll put it in my wallet and carry it in my hip pocket, right over my heart."

"You've changed, Joe," she said sadly. "You're hard. You make fun of everything. You shouldn't do that. You should believe in something."

"I do," I said, looking at my empty glass. "I believe it's time for me to take a shower and get dressed or I'll be late for my date."

It shook her up just a little, my cutting short this warm, intimate old-friends conversation because of another girl, and there was a small, sharp glitter in her smile when she asked, "Your date, is she nice, Joe?"

"Hell no. She's a mutt. I take her out only because I'm sorry for her."

"Now, Joe! What is she really like?"

I was certainly not going to discuss Claire with her. "Just medium," I said.

"Oh come, Joe, that doesn't mean anything. 'Medium' is just a face in a crowd."

"Yeah, more or less. She's only beautiful, nothing spectacular."

"As beautiful as I am?" she dared me.

I weaved inside that one and said, "You're not beautiful, you're gorgeous. You're opening tonight at the Esplanade and she isn't. That's the difference."

She mistook it for a compliment, preened a bit without moving a muscle, the way women can, and murmured, "You're sweet." But she still wasn't satisfied and persisted, "Is she someone I know, someone from the old neighborhood?" She wanted a mental picture so she could feel even more gorgeous. Her looks were her shield and sword, the weapons she had used to fight her way out of the Ironbound where she had been a wild young brat who danced jeeringly on the sidewalk with a handful of snatched grapes, daring Minotti to chase her, while five of us kids waited behind the board fence to raid the rest of his fruit bins. Her shield and sword and she guarded them jealously, as undoubtedly she had to. Without her looks she'd never have been even hat-check girl in the Esplanade, let alone the star.

Or perhaps I was misjudging her. Maybe she was genuinely interested. For the moment. Janice could be genuinely interested in a lot of odd things for the moment—she had paid some of the guys' fines when they were pulled in on minor charges, she had bought glasses for Red Murphy's kid when he was out of work, and she had paid the bills when Ellen McShane had a baby, instead of letting the girl go to the Florence Crittendon Home. Of course, it was a way of letting the rest of us know she was getting on in the world, though she had really believed she was doing good at the moment. She was a funny mixture—warmhearted, coldly ambitious, generous, greedy, spendthrift, grasping. Too bad she had those spectacular good looks; she might have been a hell of a fine girl. She had the instincts.

Still, I wasn't going to feed her vanity by discussing Claire. "You wouldn't know her," I said. "She comes from Ohio. Columbus."

"You mean the Loomis girl! But she's so—" I was sure she was about to say plain or homely or something like that, but she switched. "—so quiet-looking, not the type I thought you'd go for at all, Joe. On the other hand, you can't judge from newspaper pictures. I'd look all washed out unless I used special make-up. It's the flashbulb lighting. It gives you that washed-out appearance."

"She's a nice kid," I said, not giving her a thing.

"I'm sure she is, but shall we go? I don't want to make you late. My car's just around the corner."

I paid the bartender, who was still staring at her, and walked her around the corner. Her car was a silver-gray Jaguar. I'd been so busy looking at her, I hadn't noticed it before. I whistled.

"That looks like money," I said.

"And I love money, Joe," she said frankly and happily, "heaps of it. But come to the opening tonight. Don't disappoint me."

"I'll do my best."

"And don't order the six-buck steak sandwich," she whispered. "It's a riffle, nothing but round steak doused in meat tenderizer. Take the breast of guinea hen. It's delicious. I had it for lunch."

I wished her all the best for the opening, and then she was gone, the Jag chuckling throatily and smugly like a self-made man with money in the bank. The "ticket" was in my pocket and it felt slightly oily, though that might have been the perspiration on my fingers.

Pure gold.

Five

I hadn't called Claire since I got home. There had been interruptions but I felt guilty, as if I'd been out cheating with another woman. I called her the minute I walked into the apartment, hoping Flavin had remembered to clear the hotel switchboard so I could get through. Then suddenly, out of the mysterious mechanical clicks, buzzes and rattles, came the sound of her voice, and the remembrance of Janice diminished and faded.

Inadequately, I said, "Hi, Claire."

"Joe! I've been waiting for you to call."

"The police had your switchboard monitored."

"The police? But why—"

"Just routine," I said quickly. "How are you?"

She paused, then said, "Just numb, Joe. I don't seem to feel much of anything."

"I know. It's been a lousy day."

"Even when they told me my father was dead. It didn't seem to mean anything. Am I callous, Joe?"

"Hell no. You never knew the guy."

"I really didn't. They wanted me to identify the body but—" I could almost hear her shudder.

"They were giving you the business. How could you identify a guy you hadn't seen for twenty years?"

"That's—what I said. I wish I could cry or something, Joe, but I can't. You can't cry unless there's something, well, personal. I can't even remember what he looked like. I didn't even recognize the newspaper picture when they showed it to me. Did you see the newspaper? It was terrible. It said you were wanted by the police."

"Just for questioning. It didn't amount to anything. And I don't want to see the newspaper. That part of it's over. But listen." I had to change the subject to get her mind off it. "Would you like to have dinner with me tonight?"

"I'd do anything to get out of this hotel, Joe. It's like—a—it's so gloomy and people keep looking at me."

"And here's something else. I have a special invitation to the opening of the Esplanade House—a new night club—but we don't have to go."

"I'd like to, Joe. I don't want a wild time but—"

"We'll just sit and watch the people. Every freeloader in Newark'll be there. Hair will be let down. I got the invitation from a friend of mine. She's the featured singer. She asked us to come for moral support."

"Then of course we'll go, Joe."

"We can leave any time you say. We don't have to do any more than put in an appearance. I'll pick you up in about an hour. Okay?"

"I'll be ready. And—thanks, Joe."

I hung up. I felt good. She was the one clear, sweet note in a sour day. Janice Noonan had been a jolt and if it hadn't been for Claire, I might have picked up the torch from where I'd dropped it. I wasn't cured by a long shot. I still remembered the kisses and the furious nights and the incredible mingling of love, anger, frustration and violence. Claire was something different—I couldn't put a name to it—but Janice was a lion-taming act and I didn't want to get back in the cage.

I showered and shaved and put on a white shirt with a dark blue knitted tie and my practically new gray suit. I didn't have a tux or white tie and tails but, hell, this was only the opening of a super gin mill, not the Presidential ball. Furthermore, I didn't think Claire would have brought an evening dress along with her.

I walked downstairs, whistling. I felt like Humphrey Bogart in one of those movies where everything is real rugged for an hour, but in the last five minutes the villains get it in the neck and he goes strolling off into the sunset with the girl he really loves, like *The African Queen*. My villains weren't in the clink but I had the girl and sunsets were a dime a dozen. Then, just as I was opening the door of my old Chevvy in the parking lot behind the apartment, I heard somebody whisper, "Hey, Cap."

It was Jeff Buckley, the big drunken sailor who'd first brought the note from Harry Loomis. He was crouched in the body of my truck.

"The cops're after me, Cap. I been hiding in a movie all day."

"You damn fool," I said, leaning against the cab and pretending to light a cigarette. "There's probably a cop watching us right now."

"I didn't knock Loomis off, Cap, but what chance'll I stand if they grab me? You're the only guy I know around here."

"Do you remember what you did with that present he sent me?"

"The present?" he said blankly.

"He gave you something for me, remember?"

"Well—kind of, Cap. Yeah, and I kept thinking I had to get it to you, no matter what, but I don't know what happened to it."

"Was it a package, or what?"

"I don't know, Cap. I was in a fog. It was like this. We took on a case of bay rum at the Panama Canal and I was loaded when we hit Port Newark. The Chief didn't know because sometimes it don't show on me for quite awhile. I can hold a helluva lot of liquor."

I could believe that and I knew how they drank in the forecastle after taking on a case of bay rum at the Canal. I'd been an oiler in the black gang of the Inter-Coastal Line. When I made my trips, the most popular drink was bay rum, water and lime juice. You won't find it on the menu at the Stork Club.

But if I had any sense, I'd turn Buckley over to the cops because he was the only one who could clear me on the missing package angle. That's exactly what I should have done. I didn't owe him a thing and, when you came right down to it, his losing the present or whatever it was had landed me right in the middle of the chowder. It would help me if I turned him in, he'd be booked for murder. It would be almost the same as if I wrote the charge on the blotter myself and my conscience wasn't that tough yet.

You see, another factor had been added—Bunny Riordan. The killing of Harry Loomis had all the earmarks of a Riordan job. He wouldn't shoot a man if he could use a club. Even as a kid he had been a bloody-minded little sadist. So it was hardly a question of "who" in my mind, but a question of "why?" The "why" was the package, of course, but what was in it? What could Harry possibly have had that was valuable enough to bring on a savage killing? Yet, there was still the possibility that Bunny had finally crossed the line, graduating from mayhem to murder simply because he liked it more. In Bunny's case, it was a logical step—but that left out the missing present.

On the other hand, if Jeff Buckley had killed Harry it would have been right there on the dock when Harry was bawling him out. He'd have used his hands. He didn't need anything else. He was powerful as a steam winch.

Naturally, I didn't think about all this point by point. It was something I, well, sort of realized all in one piece.

So how could I turn Buckley over to the cops?

"Listen to me for a minute," I said without turning and looking at him behind me in the body of the truck. "You can't stay here. It's the worst place for you. I'm being watched. I know it."

"Let me stay in your joint just for the night, Cap. I ain't got no other place to go."

"And have Flavin walk in and find you there? Use your head."

"Thanks, Cap," he said in a nasty voice, "thanks

for everything."

"Don't be a jerk," I said sharply. "I wouldn't be doing you a favor, letting you stay here."

"All of a sudden you can't get rid of me fast enough. But I been thinking it over, Cap. I ain't no dummy. Mr. Loomis gave me something for you and you say I lost it. But suppose I didn't lose it. Suppose I did bring it to your joint and you stashed it away before waking me up. I've had all day to figure it out, Cap. Suppose that thing wasn't for you at all. Suppose he just wanted you to hold it for him and suppose it was worth a lot of dough and just suppose you got it in your mind to keep it for yourself. That'd change things, wouldn't it, Cap? That'd make everything different. I know what you're thinking. You're thinking, Jeff Buckley, that big slob, he's dumb enough to believe anything. Well, I ain't, Cap, and you ain't putting the boots to me neither. I don't take the fall for nobody unless there's something in it for me. So don't ask for trouble, Cap. I been pushed around enough."

"You can do as you damn well please," I said angrily. "I've warned you."

There was a creak and a rustle and I ducked just as his fist slammed into the side of the cab where my head would have been. I jumped away and whirled to face him but he remained concealed in the body of the truck. He had enough sense not to show himself.

"Get out of here, Buckley," I said. "Get out of here while it's dark. If you wait till morning, you'll be picked up. But as far as I'm concerned, they can throw you in the clink and burn the place to the ground."

"Aw, don't get sore, Cap. I lost my temper for a minute, that's all. It's been a bitch of a day. Honest to God, I wouldn't hurt you. You're the only friend I got around here. Don't throw me over, Cap. I know I'm just a dumb clunk but who knows? I might be able to do you some good some day. I ain't a bad guy, honest."

"Do yourself some good and get out of here."

As I walked over to my car he called cheerfully, "And I didn't mean none of them things I said, Cap. I know how to treat a right guy. Don't worry about nothing. We'll get out of this."

I didn't answer but, my God, if he told Flavin that perhaps he had brought the package to my apartment, there'd be all hell to pay. I wouldn't be one of the suspects; I'd be it. My hands felt clammy and slippery on the wheel as I drove away.

Flavin! I swore. I hadn't called him about Bunny Riordan. I stopped at the drug store and called him from the pay booth. He should have been off duty but he was one of those cops who keep going because they love it. Some cops turn into human beings after hours, raise kids, talk to the neighbors, grow flowers. Not Flavin. If he had an apartment or a room, he probably had it sprayed so it'd smell exactly like Headquarters.

"That's very interesting," he said after I told him about Bunny. "So he paid you two visits within twenty-four hours. A little unusual, don't you think? What was he after?"

"I couldn't get anything out of him. Maybe you can do better."

"Maybe. I don't see how he got away from you, though."

"He kicked the cocktail table in my face."

"You were holding a gun on him and he heaved a table at you. Did anyone else see him?"

"I don't know. He ran out the back way."

"That's too bad. If nobody else saw him, it's just your word against his. Suppose he claims he wasn't there at all? Then what? I can't arrest people on your say-so alone."

"You can ask around, can't you? It's a crowded neighborhood and a man running down the street would hardly go unnoticed."

"Oh, we'll investigate, Malone. Don't worry about that. You think he was after that package Loomis sent you, or that he knows something about the killing?"

"Ask him. Dig into his background." I felt as if I were talking to a brick wall. "Find out who he works for."

"We'll do all that—if there is a Bunny Riordan."

"There is one, though maybe he isn't called Bunny anymore. That was a nickname when he was a kid on account of his buck teeth. He might even have a record."

"We'll check, Malone. I'll put a man on it right away. But it's quite a coincidence, isn't it?"

"What is?"

"Well, there you are with things looking bad and just in the nick of time a funny-looking gunman with buck teeth comes along and makes all kinds of vague threats and points a gun at you. Only he gets away and you spend an hour or so talking to a couple dames before you get around to calling the police. Can you blame me for wondering what the hell *did* go on?"

"It happened just the way I told you," I said desperately. "And you saw what he did to my apartment last night."

"I saw a mess, if that's what you mean. I could have torn up the place the same way myself in ten minutes but what would it prove?"

"I still have his gun, too."

"You have *a* gun," he corrected me dryly. "And I'll bet you right now, Malone, that when we check the serial number, it'll turn out to have belonged to four other guys, all named John Smith. So far you haven't given me a thing."

"All right," I said angrily. "Forget it. Forget the whole damn thing."

"Oh no, Malone. We won't forget it. We'll look into it very carefully, if only to prove you pulled this Bunny Riordan out of the telephone book. In fact, I'm glad you called. I'm always interested to see how the minds of you guys work—and you'd be surprised, you all work about the same."

I fought my temper down, reminding myself that an investigation would surely turn up something about Bunny. He'd been a bloody-minded kid and was now a pro. It was a little reassuring to think that Bunny couldn't stand an investigation. Flavin was a cop, a real cop, and he'd find a character like Bunny interesting— maybe interesting enough to take the pressure off me. In a cockeyed way, Flavin was the friend-in-need on whom I had to count. There was nobody else.

"As long as you look into it," I said without any inflection of either anger or pleading. "I'm not asking any favors."

I walked slowly back to the car and sat for a while looking at nothing but the rim of the steering wheel. Not mulling, thinking, not planning—just sitting there, letting the cells and tissues renew themselves a little. Then I lit a cigarette and drove on to meet Claire.

Six

I was glad to find her waiting in front of the hotel for me. The lobby was so depressing with the gloom of all the dreary years that Venus de Milo herself would have looked like Boris Karloff's spinster aunt. Not Claire, of course. She'd have looked wonderful even in a pine box with rope handles. She was in a dark green something-or-other—I don't know anything about women's clothes—and looked dressy enough to go anywhere with anybody at any time for any reason, including the wedding of a movie star. She had on plain silver loop earrings, a pearl necklace, and a small tangle of thin silver bracelets on her left wrist. Her bag was made of seed pearls and was about the size of an envelope. There was a hint of strain around her eyes, but she looked lovely all the same. She gave me a small smile when I stopped at the curb. It was only after I reached over and held the door open for her that I remembered a gentleman would have gotten out of the car and assisted the lady to her seat. Not that they needed help, but they liked that little touch on the elbow as they bent over and sat down.

"I don't have any manners," I said. "But I came from a poor family. My father wore dark glasses and sold pencils for a living. My mother helped with the budget by laundering motormen's gloves. I was a juvenile delinquent and stole potatoes from the vegetable store down the street."

She laughed and said solemnly, "*My* mother made hats, which should be a criminal offense, too. Some of them looked like decorated pie tins."

Then she fell silent. I knew she was suddenly thinking of her father and I said quickly, "Well, what do you feel like—steak, fish food or spaghetti?"

To my surprise, she chose spaghetti. Most girls would have gone for the lobsters or the T-bones. We drove to the Italian Chef on Branford Place. It was one of the fancier joints but they served the best veal and peppers in the city.

"You order for me," she whispered over the table after we were seated at the big plate glass window through which you could watch the cook make pizza pies. "I've never been in an Italian restaurant before."

Grandly, I ordered the works—antipasto, minestrone, veal and peppers and a bottle of Chianti. Before dinner, we had martinis. Ordinarily, as far as I'm concerned, you can use martinis to wash the windows, but I wanted to make an impression. At first she tried to be gay but it was an effort.

"Let's just relax, honey," I said with my usual tact. "If you don't feel like talking, it's okay with me."

"It's not that, Joe. It's—oh, everything, I guess."

"I know."

"It's not what you think, Joe. It's not my father. I feel badly but, oh, I scarcely knew him and his death hasn't really touched me deeply. It's, well, I have a feeling there's something going on and I don't know what it is. Do you know what I mean?"

I thought of Bunny Riordan and my wrecked apartment and the raking-over I'd been given by Flavin and Gilman, but I couldn't tell her about that now, could I? She had troubles enough of her own, and enough grief, too.

"Well," I said vaguely, "maybe it's because you're in a strange place. I imagine it's a little different from Columbus, Ohio."

"It's not that. It's—did you see the late afternoon papers, Joe?"

"Not exactly," was my intelligent reply.

"They keep talking about what they call a mystery package." She was not happy about this at all. "They haven't come right out and accused my father of anything, but when you read between the lines you can see they think he was mixed up in something, well, illegal. He wasn't much of a father, I admit, but are they allowed to say things like that?"

"A lawyer once told me you can't libel the dead. They can print anything they want as long as it doesn't reflect on you. It seems pretty lousy, but that's the law."

"I wasn't thinking about that," she made a dismissing gesture. "Then there were those two policemen, Mr. Flavin and Mr. Gilman. They came to see me and some of their questions sounded very odd."

"In what way?" I knew the kind of questions they'd probably asked, but I had to say something.

"Well, I had the feeling they suspected me of something."

"And me, too. Right?"

"They didn't say that," she said quickly.

"But they let you know, didn't they."

"Well—" She seemed to hang unhappily on that word every time she started to say something. "They intimated that it was very strange that I should come to see you and that I should want to see my father after the way he treated mother and me. What's behind it, Joe? What did they mean? They can't possibly think—" She stopped as if the very thought were too horrible to express.

"Can't think what, honey?" I prompted her.

"That—I had something to do with his death. Of course I might be imagining the whole thing," she added hurriedly. "They didn't come right out and accuse me, you understand."

"But I was included, wasn't I?" I asked grimly.

"N-no—"

"I know they did, honey. They talked to me, too. In fact, they laid it on the line. Or almost."

She looked bleakly at me, her face drawn and her slim fingers a tight, white-knuckled knot on the lip of the table. "Isn't there anything we can do, Joe?"

"Why should we have to do anything?" I

demanded, angry in spite of not wanting to be. "I know how cops are. In a case like this, they look around for the easiest suckers. All right, they're smart. I'll give them that much. They can start with practically nothing and in the end there's a guy in the electric chair down at Trenton, and ninety-nine and nine tenths of the time they get the right one. Most cases are fairly obvious, but along comes something like this and they use the same technique—pick a couple of likely suspects and go to work on them."

"But, Joe—" Her face was ashen.

"Relax." I was far from relaxed myself. "Cops don't usually frame people, though they can be a pain in the neck while it's going on. And there's nothing we have to do, nothing at all. In fact, the best thing to do is nothing."

Man, believe me, this was a prime example of whistling as I tried to pass the boneyard. Maybe there was nothing I could do, but there was plenty Flavin and Gilman could do and I had a fairly good idea they wouldn't be ladies and gentlemen about it, either. Of course I didn't mention this to Claire.

"So don't worry, honey," I added.

She managed to smile, but that stricken darkness remained in the depths of her gray soft eyes. She was not the kind of girl who should ever have been mixed up in a thing like this.

"All right, Joe," she said.

I looked at her and a very unpleasant thought occurred to me. I had a fair idea how the police worked when they had two suspects—play one off against the other, hint at a double-cross or finally at a confession or both.

"Let's hold everything for a minute," I said bluntly. "Did they suggest I was holding out on you, that I'm giving you the runaround, that I actually did get a package from Harry and didn't tell you about it?"

I could see in her face that I had scored, but instead

of denying it she lifted her chin and said, "They tried, but I didn't believe it."

"Not even for a minute?" I pressed her. "You didn't start to wonder or anything like that? After all, I'm practically a stranger. Why should you trust me? Why should you take my word for a single, solitary thing? For all you know, I might be Jack the Ripper or somebody."

"I have no doubts about you, Joe, I have no doubts at all."

"But how can you be sure? How do you know I'm not giving you a line?"

To my astonishment, she looked hurt. "Is that what you think of me?" she asked. "Do you think I'm spying on you? That's what it would amount to, wouldn't it?"

I felt as if several steel clamps had been removed from my head, and I grinned weakly. "They really did a job on us, didn't they, Mr. Flavin and Mr. Gilman? But let's forget them before they spoil our appetites. Here comes the antipasto."

The waiter served the platter of hors d'oeuvres and I felt happier then. Somehow or other, the bond between Claire and me seemed ten times as solid, bringing with it a warm intimacy that hadn't existed before. There's an old saying, and mostly it works in reverse, but sometimes there is nothing like trouble to draw people together. Claire and I could have been at each other's throats, as Flavin intended, but instead I wanted to take her in my arms and tell the lot of them to go to hell. She was a wonderful girl. I've said that before, but the way I felt then, I wanted to have it tattooed on my chest, surrounded by a heart, clasped hands and forget-me-nots.

Dinner passed pleasantly. A gypsy-looking girl in a red skirt and a white embroidered blouse played a mandolin, while another girl, who might have been her sister, did some dances and rattled a tambourine. One of the waiters sang *O Sole Mio* and the proprietor squeezed a concertina. It was all very nice and informal, though I knew this was a regular feature of the place, so it was really planned and not informal at all.

Afterward, Claire and I strolled slowly up Broad Street looking in the shop windows, avoiding the neon fireworks of Market Street with its honkytonks, movies and cheap-drink bars. We arrived at the Esplanade House about ten o'clock.

It was jammed. People were all over the place—standing, sitting, walking, talking, drinking—and the babble was a muffled roar. There were people in evening dress, business suits and even sport clothes. The dining room was full, the bar was a madhouse, and the lobby was so packed that we had to inch our way in from the front door. You could barely hear the orchestra.

"We're not going to stay here long," I muttered to Claire. "If I want to be packed, I'll join a sardine factory."

But Janice Noonan, surrounded by several men, spied us, waved and beckoned for us to join her. Her shimmery gown was pretty sexy and at first glance she looked gold-plated, it was that tight on her. With her figure, even gold plating wouldn't have been an improvement. Yet, compared to Claire's more conservative ensemble, she looked like the featured stripper in a super-burlesque. Which was the effect intended, I suppose. After all, the ornately framed one-sheets at the foot of the marble stairs just inside the doors, billed her—and her alone—as Felice Daudet, Songs.

She hadn't been kidding when she said she knew the right people. She introduced us to Mayor Hadley; Prosecutor Leonard; Sam Crowley, manager of the place; Abe Kinney, the gambling man; Alec Curry, who ran Curry's Gym on Market Street and was also a fight promoter; and a jeweler named Stocker, who was so well known in Newark that even I recognized his name. He was a portly man with a mane of bushy white hair that made him look like a Senator. He was very polished in white tie and tails. Alec Curry was as ill-kempt and crabby as ever, but Abe Kinney, tall and slim, wore a white dinner jacket with a midnight-blue cummerbund and bow tie. His hair was the color of polished chrome and he appeared sleepy, his usual expression. Janice was flanked by Stocker and Kinney and I wondered—without any feeling about it one way or the other—which of the two was her current keeper. My guess was Stocker, because he kept cupping her elbow in his hand as if to prevent anyone from taking her away. But Kinney, I was sure, was the real owner of the Esplanade House. It wouldn't have been the first night club he had backed. And it would be successful. He was a gambler in name only. He never went into anything unless he was sure of success. There would never be enough money in the world to satisfy Abe Kinney. He liked it, he liked it in large quantities and he liked to make it.

"I'm so glad you came, Joe," Janice said warmly, just as if I were in the same financial class as the men around her. "I was counting on you. He's my luck," she told the others, "he's my magic charm. Now I know I'll go over tonight."

She was nervous and it showed in the brittle quickness of her speech.

"Of course you'll be a sensation, my dear," said Stocker elaborately. "You'll be the talk of the town, the toast of café society."

"I wouldn't have hired her if I didn't think so myself," said Kinney in a bored voice. "If this mob of high class panhandlers'll shut up long enough to let her sing, that is."

I flashed him a glance of appreciation. Kinney was all right. Nothing and nobody fooled Abe Kinney. He was a complete realist.

"You should have charged," said little Alec Curry sourly. "You should have charged fifty bucks a head and called it a preview house-warming. Now what've you got? A houseful of deadbeats."

"Publicity, Alec, publicity. Money can't buy it."

"Abe's right," the mayor informed us as if it were something he had thought up himself. "There are things money can't buy."

"It bought this mob," said Alec Curry. "I hate to think of what it's costing. And for what? Deadbeats. I wouldn't give them coffee and doughnuts."

Kinney murmured, "How right," but it went by Alec without an echo. Alec might not have been the stingiest man in Newark, but there wasn't much green left on a dollar when he parted with it. He knew his reputation and didn't care. He was reputed to be wealthy but you'd never think of it to look at his cheap baggy tweed suit. It was said he ate oatmeal three times a day because he was too miserly to buy anything more expensive. He was a tight Scotsman, all right.

Janice said hastily, "I reserved a table for you, Joe, and please, please keep your fingers crossed for me tonight. Promise?"

Her hand was on my arm and from the way she looked up at me, standing close, you'd have thought she was asking me to meet her in her apartment at midnight. But this was the brushoff. I'd known Janice Noonan for almost twenty years, ever since we were scrappy kids together Down Neck, and she couldn't fool me more than fifty per cent of the time. Still, I flushed because I had a fair idea of what the others must be thinking. Abe Kinney had one sleepy eyebrow cocked, as if amused at a bedroom revelation. Alec Curry gave me a lewd grin, Stocker frowned and Claire looked quickly from me to Janice and back again, her face suddenly expressionless. Prosecutor Leonard's glance was sharper and more intent.

"Malone," he said. "Malone ... Joe Malone. I'm

sure I heard that name recently and—"

"But really," Janice said hurriedly, smothering the rest of his observation, "Joe *is* my luck. I know that's superstitious, but I'm Irish. I believe in leprechauns, too."

"I'm her rabbit's foot," I said. "Her amputated rabbit's foot, that is."

"With your talent and personality, my dear," said Stocker in that plush upholstered voice of his, "luck—though I would call it success—will follow you wherever you go."

"She'll need more than luck tonight," murmured Kinney, glancing into the crowded, milling dining room. "She'll need a voice like a steam calliope. I'm just joking, Jan. Don't worry, we'll have quiet when you do your number."

"The only way you'll quiet that mob," said Alec Curry, "is to slip them a mickey."

I could see Janice wanted me to be on my way now—possibly because I had been recognized by the Prosecutor. Joe Malone, suspect number one in the Harry Loomis killing. She turned to Sam Crowley, manager of the club.

"Show Joe to his table, will you, Sam? He'll never be able to get through that jungle in there without a native guide."

The brushoff was complete.

Seven

There were two thickset, muscular men sitting at our table but they got up instantly and walked away when Crowley appeared with us in tow. I recognized them. They were two of the strongarms who worked for Abe Kinney in his gambling place on Frelinghuysen Avenue. We were hardly seated before a waiter came up with a champagne cocktail for Claire and a rye and soda for me.

"There will be no check tonight, sir," he said, looking at the small tray in the middle of the table. It was the kind of tray on which waiters brought your change and on which you left your tip.

After he left, Claire sipped her cocktail and said politely, "Have you known Miss Noonan long, Joe?"

I set her straight right away. I didn't want any misunderstandings. "We grew up together when I lived Down Neck. That's one of the tough sections of Newark. I went around with her for awhile but it petered out. You know how it is. You find out it isn't the same and you drift apart."

"She seemed very friendly."

"Oh, we're friends and all that. Always will be, I guess, having lived in the same neighborhood so long—I've known her almost all my life—but she went this way"—I waved my hand to indicate the night club—"and I went a half dozen other ways. It happens all the time. The old gang, some of the guys used to be my best friends but I never see them anymore."

I didn't mention that Jimmy Corcoran was in the state pen and Frankie Keogh had been knocked off in a numbers racket squabble.

Claire didn't change visibly but she stopped being so distantly polite. Not that I blamed her for chilling up on me. No girl likes being taken out just so the guy can see his other girl friend. And it was funny, after having met Claire, I felt about Janice exactly the way I said—she was just a friend from the old neighborhood. Things had petered out between us. I was cured.

Claire and I had just about started talking again in that warm, intimate way that had made dinner so pleasant in the Italian restaurant, when she broke off in the middle of a sentence, her face froze and she said, "Oh!"

But this time I had nothing to do with it. She was staring at something behind me. I turned and there was Flavin in an iron gray suit which matched his eyes.

"Hello, Malone," he said. "I didn't know you had the influence to rate that solid gold invitation. But then you used to work for Abe Kinney, didn't you?"

"You must rate with Abe yourself," I said, handing it back to him. Cops didn't rate with Kinney unless they were the Chief, the Commissioner or on the payroll.

"Me?" said Flavin, impassively sitting down on one of the two empty chairs at the table. "Abe wouldn't know me from a cigar store Indian. I just dropped in out of curiosity, Looks like a mob scene from *The Ten Commandments*, doesn't it? A regular Cecil B. DeMille orgy. Hello, Miss Loomis. Don't tell me you're enjoying this madhouse."

"We were," I said. Then bluntly, "What's on your mind, Lieutenant?"

I knew damn well he hadn't dropped in out of idle curiosity.

He lit a cigarette and blew out a lazy plume of smoke. "I'll tell you," he said. "I've got a little news item about another friend of yours. An able-bodied seaman—A.B. I think they call them—named Jefferson Buckley."

I heard Claire gasp but I was too busy watching Flavin's hard and professionally cynical face to turn to her.

"What about him?" I asked.

I hoped I sounded calmer than I felt. Something from inside me had crawled up into my throat and was squatting there as thick and clammy as a toad. In a nasty, resentful mood, such as he had exhibited once already, Jeff Buckley could really make things black and blue for me.

Flavin shrugged. "He gave himself up."

I swallowed. "He what?"

"Turned himself in. Said he heard we were looking for him and wanted to get straightened out. He had an alibi. He'd been in a Rahway gin mill all the time and the bartender confirmed it. Buckley came in drunk, passed out and slept in a back room for the rest of the night. So that clears him."

"Why tell me?"

"He's a friend of yours, isn't he?"

"I told you I never saw him before that night."

"You didn't? Now where did I get the idea you were friends?"

I waited for him to go on and finally I asked, "Is that all?"

He pretended surprise. "I don't know what you mean. Should there be more?"

"More what?"

Flavin looked at Claire's strained face and shook his head. "Maybe I'm dumb," he said, "but I'm beginning to feel as though we're going around in circles. Were you expecting more of something out of this, Malone? And don't ask me something what. You're the one who's in the know. I'm just groping around. I still have to depend on people to tell me things. Though," he added, "it won't always be like that."

He had his technique down perfect. Jab, jab, jab and keep you off balance every minute, and every once in a while a short right hook to the pit of your stomach.

But I was all right now. Flavin was crafty but he wouldn't have been so casual if Jeff Buckley told them he *had* delivered a package from Harry Loomis to me, which I wouldn't have put past Buckley for a second if he was feeling mean. So Buckley hadn't said anything and Flavin was just trying to needle me. Now that that thing was out of my throat and I could breathe again, Flavin didn't bother me. For the time being.

"All I meant," I said, "is, did you turn him loose?"

"Why not? Is there any reason why he should be in jail?"

"None that I know of. But not being a cop, I'm not up on things like that. You probably can name a half dozen charges to book him on."

"Not offhand," said Flavin. "But I will tell you one thing. If he keeps drinking at the rate he has been, he'll wind up in the alcoholic ward or worse. There's a bad streak in him, Malone, and liquor doesn't help. This isn't a guess. I could tell from talking to him. One of these days he's going to run amuck and kill everything in sight like that crazy barber in Lyndhurst a couple years ago. Nobody can predict what'll happen when your brain gets an overload of rotgut. Guys like Buckley are a menace. I mean that, so if you're fooling around with him in any way, Malone, watch your step. He'll turn on you just like that." He snapped his fingers.

All this time we had been our own little island in the midst of the crowd, some of them standing, some of them walking and some of them just milling aimlessly with a drink in their hand, hemming us in. But—and I've seen this happen with crowds before— they shifted and there was an open lane from our table to the door and as I glanced up, Bunny Riordan in a dinner jacket strolled to the entrance with a plump, skimpily-dressed little blonde on his arm and stood there for a moment. I leaped to my feet, grabbing Flavin's shoulder and pointing excitedly at the doorway.

"There, over there!" I cried. "The guy I told you

about—Bunny Riordan, there in the doorway!"

But by the time Flavin turned his head to look, the crowd shifted again and right in front of us was a wall of bare female backs and black dinner jackets. I jumped up on the chair to see over their heads but Bunny was no longer in the doorway and it was useless to try to fight through that mob. In that crush, I could have passed within ten feet of him without knowing it.

"He's gone," I said, sitting down.

"Are you sure he was there in the first place?" Flavin asked.

"Of course I'm sure. He's with a little blonde in a blue dress," but as I looked around, I knew how silly that sounded. Every other blonde was wearing a blue dress of one shade or another.

"You know," said Flavin, pushing back his chair from the table, "this Riordan of yours interests me. I've asked a dozen boys at headquarters and they never heard of him. Bunny Riordan, eh?"

"Maybe he changed his name."

"Could be," Flavin stood and ground out his cigarette in the tray before me. "Well, I'll see you around, Malone. Have a good time, Miss Loomis."

He nodded and eased himself into the crowd. Claire leaned toward me over the edge of the table.

"I don't like that man, Joe," she said in a low, troubled voice. "Is that the way policemen are—always trying to trip you up?"

"For the love of Mike, no," I said. "Some of them try to sell you tickets to the Policemen's Ball."

As a joke, I've heard funnier at funerals.

Eight

On the other hand, even if it had been as hilarious as fat Mayor Hadley in a sack race with his two-headed brother, I don't think either of us could have raised even a feeble smile. Flavin had spoiled it. He couldn't have spoiled it more completely if he had laid a cadaver in formaldehyde on the table in front of us. He had done this deliberately and for obvious reasons, although the mere sight of him would have accomplished just about the same result.

I was glum but I think Claire was a little scared. She had never been up against a situation like this before and it must have seemed like a nightmare to her. In her ordered Columbus, Ohio, existence, policemen were friendly or gave you tickets when you were naughty. Flavin was something new and frightening. She hadn't been naughty but he was after her all the same. I knew how she felt. I felt the same, and the noise and confusion and phony gaiety began to get on my nerves—and my nerves aren't easy to get on.

"Look, honey," I said, "let's get out of this squirrel cage. Let's go some place where we can have a quiet drink and listen to some decent music on the juke box, like maybe Duke Ellington, and have room to dance if we feel like it. What do you say?"

To my surprise, she shook her head. "Not until your friend sings her number."

"Janice? In this mob, she'll never know the difference."

"You promised," she said stubbornly. "And she *will* know the difference. I know I would, if I were in her place, and she will, too."

I said, "Okay," and when the waiter came around with another pair of drinks—we were getting wonderful service, considering the crush—I asked him when Janice went on. She went on at midnight, which gave us another hour in this boiler factory. I knew Claire really wanted to go but out of some kind of queer, cockeyed feminine loyalty, or whatever you want to call it, we had to sit there till Janice did her number.

As it turned out, our wanting to stay or leave didn't make any difference. Our entertainment had been planned.

The orchestra was still struggling against the mounting din but it was impossible to dance, so we sat at the table, and you know the kind of nervous brittle talk that comes out when two people are trying not to show each other how depressed they are. If I had known Claire longer, if I had been closer to her, things would have been different and there would have been more mutual sustenance. As it stood, we were really comparative strangers and I didn't know how to get to her, nor she to me. I was desperately trying to think of all the clean jokes I knew when a gaunt, sick-looking man in a gray suit, gray shirt and gray tie came to the table and mumbled that I was wanted on the telephone.

"Me?" I said in surprise. "You must have the wrong Malone, brother. Nobody'd call me here."

He said, "Just a minute," and fumbled limply in his coat pockets, bringing out an old, wrinkled envelope. "You own the Malone Building Supply Company, Two-seventeen Midland Avenue? You got a phone call then."

The only thing I could think of was that my warehouse had been broken into or was on fire or something, and almost everything I owned except the truck was there. I jumped up, said a hasty, "Excuse me a minute, honey," to Claire, and elbowed my way through the crowd behind the gaunt man.

"The front phones are all busy," he droned. "It's back here."

We went through the swinging doors past the

kitchen and he opened me into a small storage room at the far end of the corridor. It was stacked to the ceiling with cases of canned goods and liquor, and ten brand-new brooms and mops and pails were clustered in the back corner. The usually naked hundred-watt bulb in the middle of the ceiling had a shade improvised from a gallon can which had once held, according to the label, cut beets.

The gaunt man said, "In here," and stepped aside. I walked in and the door closed behind me. Of course there was no telephone, but seated on a case of evaporated milk and smoking a cigarette that smelled like a cigar was a slim, Latin-looking man with a smooth complexion the color of mellowed piano keys.

"Ah, Mr. Malone," he said pleasantly. "Please forgive my harmless little stratagem but it was of the utmost importance that I talk privately with you. The name will mean nothing, naturally, but I am Juan Garcia, at your service."

Translated, Juan Garcia was the equivalent of John Smith or Mr. Anonymous. I had lived long enough among the Portuguese, Spaniards and Cubans Down Neck to know that.

Here we go again, I thought dourly. But I wanted to hear what Mr. Juan Garcia had to say. Or rather, *how* he would say it.

"What's of the utmost importance?" I asked.

He smiled and waved a slim, graceful hand. "Please make yourself comfortable, Mr. Malone. I am sorry there are no easy chairs but I can offer you a case of asparagus. Or do you prefer the tomato juice? I'm afraid my small jokes are not very amusing, are they?"

"Did you bring me here to make jokes?" I sat watchfully on the case of asparagus within reaching distance him.

"No indeed. I will come immediately to the point. I have been delegated to make you a substantial offer for the package sent to you by Mr. Harry Loomis. You yourself will not be able to obtain any profit from it and it may even prove an embarrassment."

"What's in it?" I asked.

"That I do not know, Mr. Malone. I am not the true owner, you understand. But you would be more aware of the contents than I, no?"

"I don't have the package."

He murmured, "Ah?" but obviously did not believe me. "Permit me to give you the history of this—merchandise, shall we call it? Yes. I am an unimportant member of a certain political party. The name of the party and of what country will not interest you. Furthermore, it is a matter of urgent secrecy. Our poor country is controlled by a most corrupt, unscrupulous and merciless man and his associates. He would not hesitate to send assassins even to here in your *Estados Unidos* if he learned of our existence. To eliminate this man and his companions, much money is necessary and many means must be employed to raise funds. You understand this, of course. Campaign funds, no?"

"This package must be worth plenty, then," I said.

"But only in the proper hands, Mr. Malone," he told me quickly. "To you and me it would be worthless and very probably a source of danger. In activities of this sort, experience and caution are of the highest importance, and I stress experience."

"It's beginning to sound to me," I drawled, "as though this thing is a load of drugs. Heroin, at a rough guess."

He held up horror-stricken hands, palms toward me. "Please, *señor!* My compadres may be guilty of smuggling, yes, but they are patriots, not criminals *viciosos*. This money we obtain is for the salvation of my poor unhappy country, but to obtain it through a viciousness is unthinkable. We are men of honor, Mr. Malone!"

Mr. Juan Garcia was all right, a first-class salesman—but I wasn't in the market. I didn't believe a word about his poor, unhappy country and the noble patriots. If there was any profit to be made, I was damn sure it was for the benefit of Garcia & Company. And as for their being men of honor, well, I'd hate to have to depend on it.

"But enough of political philosophy," he said, smiling. "I have learned in your country to be practical. You are thinking to yourself, of what benefit is this to me, no?"

"Yes," I said.

"Ah," he was now pleased with himself, "I have learned well, you see? So now down to the business. As ethics, Mr. Loomis purloined the package and it should be restored to us, the rightful owners, but we are not dealing with ethics. One cannot eat ethics or buy a new house with them. So much for the ethics. If you restore to us the package, Mr. Malone, we in turn will do this for you. I cannot offer to you the reward of money but I can promise to you two trucks, a large one and a small one. This will be from a fellow-countryman who is in the business. He will be rewarded later with a post in the government when we are successful. That has already been understood."

"Two trucks yet. That's pretty good. They'll come in handy, real handy."

Sarcasm was wasted on him.

"We thought of that, *señor*," he said modestly. "In an agreement among gentlemen, the values are always to be observed."

"Sure, but what kind of trucks will they be? You said a large one and a small one, but that doesn't mean anything. Can I tell you what I want?"

"Of a certainty, *señor*. My compadres will arrange it."

That was the tipoff on that deal. If his compadre was in the new- or used-truck business, he'd have to have a lot as big as Secaucus to give me that much of a choice. They either did not intend to give me any trucks at all—and where would I wind up with my throat cut?—or they planned to steal a couple for me. So the men of honor were planning to present me with an 8-ball.

But I didn't care about that. I wanted to find out who, what, when, where and why to get myself off the hook, so I went along with him.

"As I told you," I said, "I don't have this package, but I might be able to get it."

"That also has been taken into consideration, *señor*."

"You think of everything. But there's something else. The killing of Harry Loomis can't be left dangling."

"The man was a thief. He knew the risk he was taking. I feel no sympathy for him."

"The hell with sympathy. I want to know what's going to be done about it."

He frowned. "I do not understand, *señor*."

"It's very simple. Cops don't look at things the way you do. They don't like people to be knocked off, even if they're thieves. When there's a murder, they want to put somebody in the electric chair for it. This may seem unreasonable, but that's the way they are. And I don't like electric chairs. Now do you understand?"

"But of course, Mr. Malone. It is very simple. If the *policia* have someone else, they will not annoy you further, no? Dismiss it from your mind. It will be arranged."

"I don't want it 'arranged.' I want them to have the guy who killed Harry."

"But naturally, Mr. Malone. I meant nothing else. The man is of no importance and I, personally, myself, will be pleased to be rid of him. It was a shameful act, the killing, of the most stupidity, and I agree the man should be punished. My superiors also agree. That is what I meant when I assured you it will be arranged. We are very angry with this man."

"But Bunny Riordan won't like it," I said. "If he talks, there might be fireworks."

He leaned toward me. "*Perdón?*" he said politely.

"Bunny Riordan, the guy who killed Harry."

"I am very sorry, *señor*, but I do not know this Bunnay Ree-dan. Mr. Loomis was killed by a countryman of mine, stupid and animal, too brutal to be trustworthy. A patriot, yes, but dangerous to us. It is unfortunate, but his zeal cannot be controlled. His only thought is that of vengeance. However, such is his love for his unfortunate, suffering country that he will go freely to the police when it is explained to him that in doing so he will best serve the Cause."

"Who is he?"

"Please, *señor*. Of such is the political secrecy," he said meaningfully, "that even the hint of disclosure or betrayal is not to be borne. I deplore the necessity, but of such is the urgency that assassins must be employed. I myself am in constant danger."

"Maybe, but I can take care of *my*self, Garcia."

"Ah yes. Our inquiries have established your fistic abilities but"—he showed a gun in his hands as if it were a card trick—"sometimes ability is not enough."

I kicked it out of his hand before he could point it, caught it in the air and put it in my pocket. He stifled a groan but held his hand to his stomach.

His smile was strained, but he said reproachfully, "I did not intend to use it, Mr. Malone. I was merely illustrating a point."

"I got the point," I said.

"You misunderstood, I assure you. If you don't mind, may I have the gun, please?"

"I'd just as soon keep it, if you don't mind."

He sighed, still hugging his kicked hand to him. "*De nada*. Consider it a gift. The pistols are very valuable to us, but it is yours."

He was damn right it was mine. After flashing it like that, did he think I was going to hand it back to him? "Is there anything else?" I asked. "I have a lady waiting for me."

"That is all, *señor*. Unless you—but how unlikely—you have the contents of the package with you."

"How can I get in touch with you?"

"Do not trouble yourself, Mr. Malone. We will establish contact with you. *Adios. Perdón—hasta la vista*, until I see you again."

There was a brief glitter in his black eyes and I knew he did not love me.

"Till we meet again," I said, and walked out—but with the uneasy feeling that I had made a mistake, a bad mistake, somewhere along the line.

When I got back to the table, Claire was sitting there rigidly, white-faced and in a state of almost frozen hysteria.

"I want to leave, Joe," she said jerkily. "I want to leave right away. I want to get out of here."

"But—what's the matter, honey?" I stammered.

"I'll tell you outside. Let's go, please!"

I said, "Sure," and led her out, shouldering and butting my way through the crowd. Alec Curry, chewing sourly on a frayed cigar butt, was standing alone in the lobby and stopped me on my way out to the front door. I didn't want to talk to him, but he had me by the forearm.

"Hold on a minute, sonny," he said. "You used to work for me, didn't you?"

"I was only one of the sparring partners at the gym," I said, trying to edge away from him.

But he clung tightly and moved closer. "What kind of trouble you in, sonny?" he asked in a low voice. "Police trouble?"

I stopped edging away. Both Claire and I could use a friend like Alec. At this point, we could use any friend at all.

"Something like that," I said.

"I know, I know. I heard them talking. You have

anything to do with it, sonny?"

"Not a damn thing, no."

"Ha!" he turned his head and spat contemptuously into the potted fern at the turn of the wall. "I'm wise to them, sonny. What they want is a patsy. Well, don't let them get away with it, mind?"

"What can I do about it?"

"Fight 'em, that's what, fight 'em. Don't let them walk all over you. And if you need help, call on me, mind? I know a few people myself. Aye, and a little money too, if you need it. Not much, mind you, times are lean, but some, but some. I take care of me own, sonny, fighters and the likes of the rest of you as can't always take care of theirself. They call me a miser, but it fair gravels me t' see 'em putting it on a feller just because he's been in the ring. Come trouble, sonny, you call on me, mind? Ha! There's nothing I'd like better than shove it down their throat. Alec Curry the miser. I'll show 'em, sonny, I'll show 'em. I got friends meself, and bigger than Mr. Prosecutor Leonard, him and his snotty remarks. You call on me now, mind? I'll settle with 'em."

I said, "Thanks, Mr. Curry, I might have to do just that."

Then he had to go and spoil it a little. His narrow, hard-bitten face took on a thin, suspicious expression and his voice turned whiny and complaining as I had heard it do so often down at the gym when he thought somebody was going to put the bite on him.

"It's not that I begrudge you the money, sonny, but it's not coming in the way it used to. I'll do all I can, mind you, and you won't have to do any more than give me your note of hand for anything I put out, but I'm dreadful short meself, dreadful short. Cash is something it ain't easy to come by, 'specially when you got it tied up here and there and only dribbles coming in. But if you need, say, fifty dollars, I'll scare it up for you some way. Though there's something better than money, sonny. It's the people you know and I know a few where it'll do the most good. State Representative McKechnie, he's a kind of cousin and a lawyer in the bargain. You see what I mean, sonny? A little help from the right quarters is better than all the money in the world."

Then, as if afraid I'd take him up on that fifty-dollar offer then and there, he patted me on the arm, said, "You can count on Alec Curry, sonny, if only because Mr. Prosecutor Leonard is a dirty Republican, hobnobbing with all them rich high-society robbers from Forest Hill. Take care of yourself, sonny, and if it gets too thick, call on me." Patting me on the forearm again, he nodded significantly, turned and burrowed into the crowd, which was now noisier and more boisterous than ever. A quadrupled crew of waiters had been passing among them with huge trays of drinks for hours.

Still, for all his eccentricity with money, Alec Curry was not an ally to disdain, and I turned to exult a little with Claire, knowing it would make her feel better. She had been right beside me, but now she was gone. I bulled my way to the street door, trailing a string of indignant protests from jostled merrymakers, and ran outside. Claire was half way up the block, looking around distractedly as if searching for a cab. I called and ran to her, taking her arm.

"The car's down this way, honey," I said soothingly, but wondering what had gotten her into this state.

"Take me home, Joe," she said, on the verge of active hysterics. "Take me back to the hotel. This horrible place. I hate it. I want to go back to Columbus. I don't like it here. I hate it. I'm going back to Columbus. I've never been in a place like this before. Take me back to the hotel."

I said sure, honey, sure and turned her toward the street on which I had parked the car, talking at every step. I don't know what I said—it didn't really make any difference at this point, I was just trying to quiet her with the lulling tone of my voice. The moment she was in the car, she burst into tears and covered her face with her hands, refusing to talk to me and pulling away, huddling in her corner, when I touched her. On West Market Street there was a drug store that stayed open sometimes till after midnight and I drove there as quickly as I could, arriving just as the druggist was locking the front door. I'd known him for years—his name was Frank Roach and I'd gotten him a real bargain in fixtures when he put in the soda fountain.

"What's the matter, for the love of Pete?" he asked. "Have an accident or something?"

"Nothing like that, Frank, but I've got a girl in the car and she's all upset. Give me a couple of those tranquilizing pills, will you?"

"Upset about what?" He gave me a good-naturedly lascivious grin.

"No, no, it's not what you think. In fact, I don't know what it is, myself. I think somebody gave her a bad time, her father was killed the other day, and maybe it's just catching up with her. I want her to get some sleep tonight."

He didn't waste any more time with remarks, but said quietly, "Sure, Joe," and walked to the back of the store. He was one nice guy. He came back with a dozen little green pills in a box and a glass of water.

"Give her two of these now and one three times a day thereafter. They're harmless, a blend of barbiturates. In twenty minutes she'll smooth right out."

I went to the car and opened the door, but before I could open my mouth, she looked at the two little pills on the palm of my hand and said sharply, "What's that?"

"Just a little something to quiet you, honey. The druggist said they're harmless and—"

"I don't need them, thank you."

"But, honey—"

"Will you please take me to my hotel or do I have to call a taxi?"

I said, "Okay, honey," and took the glass of water back to Frank Roach.

"Don't force her, Joe," he said. "Put the box of pills in her handbag. I wrote the directions on the cover. Let her take them by herself. They won't hurt her."

I said, "Thanks, Frank. You're a pal," and, returning to the car, drove Claire to her hotel. She opened the door but I reached across her and closed it again.

"Now what's the matter?" I asked. "What happened?"

She tilted her chin and stared straight ahead through the windshield. "You should know."

"Know what?"

"That alleged phone call, Mr. Malone. There wasn't any, was there?"

"No. I'll tell you about it if you want, but I'd rather wait till tomorrow and—"

"Of course there wasn't any phone call. You were with that woman in her dressing room backstage."

"For the love of Mike," I said incredulously. "Where'd you get *that* idea?"

"What you do is entirely your own affair, Mr. Malone, but I don't like to be used."

"I didn't see her, honey—"

"Please. I'm not interested. Nor do I like to be called honey."

This was out of all proportion and I said slowly, "What's the rest of it, Claire? What else happened? Who was talking to you while I was away?"

I could see I scored but it wasn't just a lucky bull's-eye. She wasn't the kind of girl who'd have backfired like this merely on account of Janice Noonan. She had been frightened by something or somebody.

"Who was it?" I repeated. "We were given the treatment tonight whether you know it or not. Me, too. I got my sales talk from a character named Juan Garcia. Who gave you yours?"

She was about to reply coldly, but compressed her lips and looked at me with narrow eyes. "It was a Mr. Brown. He came to the table after you left. He said you and my father were in a deal together but something went wrong and you abandoned my father and let him get killed after you got what you wanted. That package."

I wasn't taken aback. I'd expected something like this. "What'd he look like, this Mr. Brown?"

"He was the man you were trying to get in trouble with the police."

That did surprise me. "The one with buck teeth? Bunny Riordan?"

"He said you approached him two months ago and asked him to go into this deal with you, but he turned you down and you've been trying to get him in trouble ever since. And he said you're cheating me of my father's share of the money you made on the deal."

I didn't argue with her. It would have done no good and might even have made her still more hostile.

"Is that what you think, too?" I asked.

She bit her lip and looked down at her clenched hands in her lap. "No," she said finally. "I don't think so."

"Then what do you think?"

Her hands became twisted little knots and she burst out, "Oh, leave me alone, will you? Just leave me alone! I don't want to think about it or talk about it or have anything to do with it. I just want to be left alone!"

She twisted in the seat, thrust the door open, sprang from the car before I could stop her and ran across the sidewalk and disappeared into the hotel. I made no move to follow her. I just sat there, staring heavily at nothing at all. She hadn't told me everything. I knew that. None of this could have frightened her as badly as she had been. In a way, she was just an ordinary kid and she had led the usual half-sheltered kind of life most girls lead, nothing violent or terrifying ever happening to them; but all the same she was not the kind of girl who surrendered easily to hysterics. I had seen how she behaved under pretty rough circumstances and she had taken all of it without a whimper.

So what else had Bunny Riordan said to her? Had he threatened her? I didn't think so. But, with the pitch he gave her about me, he had built up to something, something that had horrified her, scared her.

The police. That would be it. With her quiet, conventional background, any other kind of threat would have seemed unbelievable, fantastic, but the police was something she could understand. Now I'd gotten that far, I could almost hear Bunny Riordan saying, "The cops have been after you, haven't they? It's been one question after another and they don't believe a thing you say, do they? You know why? Malone. He's tough and he'll throw anybody to the cops to get off the hook himself. You, me, anybody. He's tried it with me already and you're next on the list. You don't have to believe me, but just think back and ask yourself why the cops asked you all those questions. Go ahead."

To a girl like Claire, such a thing would be a nightmare. Then, too, the past few days had also been pretty horrible and she was ripe for panic.

She'd feel better in the morning after she had time to think and was rested I told myself.

When I got back to my apartment, I discovered that I still had the box of pills, so I took three and went to bed. Within twenty minutes I was drifting into a soft, cushioned chemical lotus land.

Nine

My truck burned that night and by the time Bivens, the janitor, excitedly woke me up there was nothing to do but stand groggily to one side while the firemen sprayed the smoking, twisted ruin with carbon tetrachloride.

"That was touched off on purpose," the fire chief told me flatly. "It stinks of kerosene. I'll have to report it. I supposed you're insured."

"Yeah, it's insured," I said.

"Well, that's between you and the insurance company. They'll get a copy of my report."

I turned away without answering. I was sick and tired of official suspicion and veiled accusation, and at that point I frankly didn't care if he did half think I set the fire myself. I was dopey from the pills and nothing mattered very much. I trudged upstairs. It was four-thirty. I made a cup of coffee, sat down at the kitchen table and stared at it without interest. The phone rang at five and I let it ring ten times before I finally roused myself and plodded across the room to answer it. It was Juan Garcia.

"Mr. Malone," he said, "I have called to apologize for this unspeakable thing that has happened. Your truck. It is inexcusable. I cannot apologize sufficiently. I am desolate."

"So it was you," I said. "The cops'll be glad to hear it."

"Please, Mr. Malone. I beg you. No one regrets it more than I and restitution will be made, I promise you. Full restitution."

"Take it up with the insurance company."

"Ah, you are furious. I do not blame you. I also am furious. It was the work of a few hotheads in the organization and they will be severely reprimanded, I assure you. It is not easy to control such people. The

Latin temperament, you understand, is sometimes highly emotional and violent. And unpredictable, Mr. Malone, unpredictable and savage."

I gripped the phone tightly. "Is this another way of saying I might be the next to get it in the neck? Was the truck just a warning, Mr. Garcia? Is that the idea?"

"No no no, Mr. Malone. You understand this thing was done without approval and the culprits will be punished."

"Send them over here. I'll be glad to take care of it for you."

"Ah, I wish that were possible, Mr. Malone, but this is a purely internal matter. But to digress, have you given any thought to our little conversation of last night? To quote, time is of the essence and—"

"Drop dead," I said, and hung up.

The phone rang again almost immediately but I plodded back to the sofa and crouched over the coffee until it rang itself out. Much more of Mr. Juan Garcia's Latin malarkey and I'd turn emotional, violent, unpredictable and savage myself.

After awhile I roused myself, took a shower, dressed, drank a pair of raw eggs in milk flavored with powdered coffee for breakfast, and went downtown to hire a U-Drive truck. I didn't feel like working but there was a delivery I had to make to a contractor. He was counting on the materials and I couldn't afford to disappoint him. I was in a funny kind of spot— competing all the time with the established supply houses. I dealt chiefly in used or superficially damaged building supplies and had no regular source for purchasing. I had to pick up the stuff where I could— a few gross of electrical fixtures from a guy who was going out of business, a half dozen hot water heaters scratched in freight handling, things like that. I had to depend on personal contact, good will and a knack for bargaining, because there were no fixed prices in that market. So I had to be on the ball all the time or lose my shirt. I did business mostly with the cheap builders and one passed the word to another, and that was the way I kept going. That's why I couldn't afford to fluff a delivery. The word would go around I wasn't dependable and that'd be that.

I called Claire's hotel around ten-thirty and after hanging anxiously on the phone for three or four minutes, I was told she did not wish to be disturbed. I hung up, doggedly resolved not to be depressed.

I completed my delivery at eleven and took the truck back to the U-Drive people. I was in no mood to haggle over prices with jobbers or contractors and I'd do myself more harm than good if I tried to keep working.

As you might expect, this thing about Harry Loomis was pressing heavily on me and I couldn't let it get me down. I had to do something about it. I sat in the car and smoked three cigarettes, wondering where to start and what to do, and then I thought of Groff, third mate on the *Tranoco*. I didn't think he knew anything but there was a chance he could fill me in with a little background on Harry Loomis. When you came right down to it, I actually knew very little about Harry. We'd gotten soused together seven or eight times, but I didn't really know the guy at all.

I drove out to Port Newark. It was lunchtime and the longshoremen were sitting around in the shade, eating thick sandwiches out of their lunch cans and drinking coffee from thermos bottles, playing rummy while they ate. The dock to which the freighter was tied was stacked with bright, fresh-smelling pine planks and the boat itself was still heaped. Nobody stopped me when I walked up the gangplank of the black and red boat. Another group of longshoremen, playing pinochle in the shade amidships, told me, after some argument among themselves, that I might find Groff on the poop deck, aft. I climbed over the mountains of lumber and there was Groff on the stern under a rigged awning of canvas, polishing his sextant.

"Oh, you're the fellow who was here the other night," he greeted me, taking the pipe from his mouth. "Malone? Yes, Malone. Wasn't that a terrible thing about the Chief? My God. Sit down. What's on your mind?"

"I wanted to talk to you about Loomis, if you have few minutes," I said, sitting on a thick coil of hawser beside him. He was younger than I remembered him, square-faced, serious, blond, but third mates are usually pretty young.

"All the time in the world," he said. "But I've told the police everything I know."

"This is something different. I've got some cockeyed idea that maybe the killing had to do with something that happened on the trip. I know this doesn't sound like much but I'm trying to unravel it."

He looked interested but said, "Nothing happened on the trip. It was the same as usual—rough in the Caribbean, hot in the Canal Zone, ground swells in the Pacific—nothing out of the ordinary."

"I was thinking of Loomis himself."

"He was the same, too. Grouchy." Then quickly, "Not meaning to speak ill of the dead."

"Was he any grouchier than usual?"

"Well ..." He took his pipe from between his teeth again and frowned at the bowl. "I don't know. He was always pretty grouchy."

"Did you know he had arthritis?"

"He did? Say now, come to think of it, I did notice he walked with a limp. And yeah, he was a little worse this last trip. Bite your head off at the least word. Very nervous." His tanned forehead clenched with concentration as he thought back. "Crabbier than hell, 'specially before we went through the Canal. I didn't pay too much attention, thinking maybe it was the heat. It was a blister, this last trip."

"How was he after you went through the Canal?"

"Oh … I didn't see him much, to tell you the truth. He spent a lot of time in his cabin when he wasn't on watch, but I did notice, now that you mention it, he did look sick after we made port, sick and crabby. Nobody wanted to cross him and one of the deckhands said he had a gun in his back pocket, but you know deckhands, they're worse than a bunch of old women. Yeah, he was really worse this trip, mister, now you recall it to me."

I felt a prickle of excitement and anticipation as if all I had to do was reach out and grasp what I was after. I don't know if you've ever felt it, but it's as if suddenly everything is clearer and more sharply in focus.

"The Canal Zone," I said. "What port did you touch—Balboa or Colon?"

"Port? We don't touch any port, mister. We anchor outside and go straight through when it's our turn. We come straight from Aberdeen, Washington, and don't tie up till Port Newark. This is a freighter, not a cruise boat, mister."

My fine, high, inspired intuition collapsed like a busted basketball. I had been sure they'd have made port at either Balboa or Colon.

"But that's on the way back," I said, clinging to the now forlorn hope of—well, I don't know what. "The trip out. Where's your first stop?"

His answer scotched that one, too.

"San Pedro, California. From there to San Francisco and then to Aberdeen for the lumber."

Now I was completely deflated. None of those ports could account for Harry's actions at the Canal. Why had he been so jittery at the Canal? It didn't make sense if they didn't touch port. They'd had to have made port at the Canal if Harry's jitters there had any significance. But they hadn't, and I knew these freighters had a schedule as unvarying as the bus between Newark and Perth Amboy. If they went straight through the Canal once, they went straight through every time. This wasn't a tramp outfit with scratch cargos for here, there and everywhere. The Trans-Ocean Line worked on contract. Still, I was sure the Canal had something to do with it.

Now I was shooting in the dark and asked, "How many trips did you make with Harry, Mr. Groff?"

"Three, all told."

"And was he always the same at the Canal?"

Groff was a slow thinker and took time before he answered. You could almost see his mind ticking off the time, day by day, casting back into the past trips. He frowned out over the oily chop of the bay, holding his pipe in his right hand.

"I always put it down to the heat," he said at length. "If you ever been through the Canal, you know it gets so bad sometimes you can't put your hand to the rail, and the Chief, he seemed to feel it more than most. Leastways, like I said, that's what I put it down to. But yeah, he was usually worse at the Canal, crabbier'n the dickens, you couldn't talk to him no ways. He was better after we got into the Caribbean."

"On all three trips he was this way? At the Canal, I mean."

"Well, more or less, yes."

It didn't make sense. It didn't make any sense at all. They went through the Canal without touching port, Harry was all wound up before, but calmed down afterward. I didn't get it. If there was a connection— and there had to be—it was beyond me.

What took place at the Canal? What was the significance? Who, what, when, where, why? It was still chasing itself around in my mind like a crazy squirrel with a toothache in its tail when I drove back to Newark fifteen minutes later.

I was picked up on South Broad Street almost the moment I came through the underpass from the highway. Flavin and Gilman. The police car drew up beside me and Flavin curtly motioned me to the curb. I stopped and the pair of them came marching back to me, Gilman about a half pace behind Flavin. But then Gilman was only a sergeant and Flavin was a lieutenant. Flavin slid into the seat beside me and Gilman stood outside, listening at the open window.

"I hear you were out to Port Newark," Flavin said with no preliminary. "Third Mate Groff called me. He seemed to think there was something funny about all those questions you asked him. And so do I. What was the big idea? He's our witness and I don't want you fooling around him. Is that plain enough?"

It had gotten so that the mere sound of his hard-jabbing voice could raise my temper several degrees, but I clenched my teeth and held on, knowing that getting me sore was one of his prime objectives. Also, there was the remote chance he might be able to see things my way for once.

"I wasn't fooling around," I said. "I had an idea but can't make heads or tails out of it. Maybe you can."

"This should be good," he said cynically. "But go ahead. I'm interested in anything you have to say, Malone. The more you talk, the better I like it. What's the pitch this time?"

I took a breath to hold down my black Irish temper and as stolidly as I could told him how Harry Loomis had been acting at the Canal—nervous and irascible before the boat went through but easing off afterward as if a touchy and dangerous business had been completed.

"But here's what I can't figure out," I said. "The boat doesn't touch port and nobody comes aboard except the Canal officials and you can't monkey with those boys. Furthermore, their business is with the captain and somebody would be sure to catch on if the first mate horned in trip after trip."

Flavin looked at me, his mouth bunched. "What am

I supposed to do?" he asked. "Congratulate you?"

"I was just telling you, damn it!"

"Telling me what? All you've said is that nothing could possibly have taken place at the Canal. In fact, you've proved it. So what's the point?"

I slumped a little in my seat and gripped the steering wheel. There was no use trying to tell him anything. Not that he was stupid—far from it—but he turned everything I said against me. Still, I wanted him to know. I had to go through with it. Maybe he'd think about it and start to wonder. He was trained for this kind of work and might be able to see something I couldn't.

"I know there's a point," I persisted, but without much hope. "I knew something about Harry Loomis. Not much, but a little. He wasn't the nervous type, so why at this particular place every trip did he get the jitters? What was the reason? And this last trip he was worse than ever."

"The heat," said Flavin, echoing Groff. "And you can't make anything more out of it than that. You've been bringing up one side issue after another, but it doesn't work, Malone. You can twist and turn and dodge all you want but in the end it always comes down to the same thing. You're being backed into a corner and you don't know what to do. But keep it up. I don't mind. I'm getting closer all the time and you know it."

I had intended telling him about Juan Garcia but I closed my mouth, knowing what he'd make of that one. "Think what you want," I said, "but you're missing something all the same."

"Oh, I don't think so, Malone. We're doing all right. And say, I hear your truck burned up last night. The fire chief says somebody touched a match to it. This wouldn't be another side issue of yours now, would it?"

"I was asleep when it happened," I said shortly.

"You don't say. Any idea who touched it off?"

"No."

He smiled remotely. "You're lying by the clock but that's all right. The more the merrier, as they say. They catch up with you, too. How're you getting along with Janice Noonan, by the way?"

"Fine."

"I'm glad to hear it. You've got some pretty stiff competition there. Who's paying her rent these days, Sergeant? Is it Stocker, the jeweler, or maybe Abe Kinney?"

"Both of them," said Gilman. "She puts out for anybody with a bank account. It used to be Jack Garrity at City Hall, but he got sent up on an election fraud."

"A high-class tramp, eh, Sergeant?"

"Yeah. Expensive."

"I think you're being a sucker, Malone," said Flavin, shaking his head. "You can't afford a chippie like that, not on the kind of money you've been making. I know she must have something pretty special, but you're headed for trouble if you try to keep up with the big spenders like Stocker and Kinney. Take my advice and call it off before there's nothing anybody can do for you."

"Thanks."

"I mean it, Malone. You'll be better off with somebody like that Claire kid from Columbus, Ohio, a clean decent girl. Let me put it this way. For the sake of argument, let's say you didn't have anything to do with the Loomis killing. It looks bad for you, I admit, but let's just suppose. But let's say you and Loomis were in this business deal and now you've got hold of the whole jackpot. Okay. You try to make time with La Noonan and what happens? She takes you for everything you've got and when it's gone, you get the kiss-off. Furthermore, you're in deeper behind the 8-ball. The deal was shady somewhere along the line and the killing is still open. See what I'm getting at? By trying to cash in, you're making yourself the fall guy, whereas if you come in today and talk to me or the prosecutor and tell us the whole story, including who else might have been in the deal, the chances are your name won't even be put on the blotter. And believe it or not"—he tapped my knee—"this is the best advice anyone ever gave you."

"I wasn't in any deal with Loomis," I said woodenly.

"Have it your own way," he slid out of the car and leaned in at the window. "But think it over. Think it over seriously. Don't make a sucker out of yourself."

He nodded once and they walked back to the police car. I thought of driving down to the gym to see Alec Curry. I needed help, but what could I say to him? Flavin was right. I had proved almost conclusively that nothing could have taken place at the Canal. I had nothing more than a hunch, backed up with the single and possibly far-fetched fact that Harry had not acted normally, and what did that amount to? A bagful of smoke.

I drove back to the apartment.

Ten

Jeff Buckley was sitting on the edge of the sofa, flipping a well-honed switchblade knife into the coffee table, which he had set up on end for a target. He gave me a narrow, lopsided grin and his first words were, "You need a better lock on that door, Cap. I can open this one with my teeth."

"Get the hell out of here," I said.

"Uh-uh." He flipped the knife again and the point thunked solidly into the wooden top of the table. He jerked it out, closed it and put it in his pocket. "Things are different now, Cap. I got the cops off my tail and you and me're getting together."

"There's only one thing you're getting," I said, "and that's out. Beat it, and I mean right now."

"You don't want to make me sore now, do you, Cap?"

"It'll be a pleasure."

"That's no way to talk, Cap, not to an old pal like me, that's no way at all."

He'd been drinking but he wasn't drunk, and behind his grin he was in a thin-eyed, ugly mood. Well, so was I and I didn't care how big he was. I started across the room and he rose lazily from the sofa to meet me. I feinted a left and hit him hard on the side of the jaw with a short right hook. He didn't even blink. He laughed and as I sidestepped to throw another right, he put out his foot and tripped me. Before I could recover my balance, he had both my arms in his huge hands, digging his fingers into the muscles. I'm no lily, but the pain of it raised me up on my toes. I weigh a hundred and eighty-five but he held me out at arm's length and, still grinning, lifted me clear from the floor and held me there. I kicked wildly for his crotch but he turned my foot with the side of his thigh.

"If I wanted to, Cap," he said unpleasantly, "I could pull the muscles out of your arms like spaghetti. You want I should do that?"

I believed him. Sweating, I managed to say, "All right, you've made your point. We'll talk it over."

"Well now, that's more like it." He set me down and gave me a casual shove that sent me staggering against the wall. "If you want to try it again, okay, only the next time I might not go so easy with you. Make me sore and I'll bust you up like an egg crate. Now put something in a glass for me. I ain't had a drink for an hour."

I didn't argue. I went into the kitchen, wishing I had a gallon of mickeys to feed him. I filled a water tumbler with straight rye and gave it to him, controlling the urge to make another try for his chin but short of using a sixteen-pound sledge, I don't think I could have made a dent in him. And all this time, mind you, the radio was blasting away with the kind of hillbilly music which sounded like a machine shop at capacity production. A drill press in my brain couldn't have been worse.

"Turn that damn thing down," I said.

His unpleasant grin didn't change. "Leave it on, I like it. It reminds me of a little old fat whore I used to know back in Tacoma. She always had the radio on and you should have heard her holler when I put it to her. You'd of thought I was using a club. She was the best old whore I ever had but she sure could holler. They tried to put me out one night and I threw the whole damn house in the middle of the street. I damn near died, watching them run bare-ass in the hedges. Funniest thing you ever saw. They never opened up again and I sure did miss that dame. *Nobody* could holler the way she did."

Now I was beginning to understand what I had on my hands. He wasn't rational. Maybe he'd always been little crazy and the Niagara of liquor he'd been pouring into himself was making him worse.

"What do you want to talk about?" I asked carefully.

"Money." He sprawled comfortably on the sofa, throwing off two of the back cushions to give himself more room. "I been working like a son of a bitch all my life and I ain't never had more than a double sawbuck in my pants at any one time. You call that living?"

"You spend it as fast as you make it," I couldn't help saying.

"Sure I spend it. What do you think I do with it, put it in my coffee like sugar? But it ain't right, work, work, work all the time and never having nothing. I'm fed up and this time I want my share and I'm getting it, understand?"

"Your share of what?"

"Don't give me that stuff, Cap," he said angrily. "You know my share of what. Harry Loomis. How much was in that package I brung?"

What I would have given right then for a nice solid Stillson wrench but there was nothing heavy enough in the apartment to use for a weapon. I could feel the cold, probing perspiration fingering my ribs.

"You didn't bring the package, remember?"

"You're a liar. He gave it to me and I brung it."

I didn't contradict him outright. He was in a dangerous, lowering mood and I was honestly afraid of him, the same as I'd have been afraid if I were penned up in a barn with a demented bull.

"Now hold on for a minute, Jeff," I said, feeling my way. "You're intelligent. You can figure things out for yourself. Would I still be in this crummy apartment if I had the money to get out? Take a look at the place. It's a dump. If I had the money, I'd be riding around in a Cadillac, not living here."

That, thank God, was something he could understand and a look of bafflement began to seep into his eyes.

"But I had the thing he gave me," he said uncertainly. "I know I had it and I remember thinking to myself I had to get it to you, no matter what. It was on my mind, soused as I was. I had to get it to you, see? I *had* to."

"Why?" I asked.

"You didn't know the Chief," he said uneasily. "Not that I was afraid of him, understand? I could of busted him with one hand. But I said I'd get it to you and I keep my word, so don't get the idea I was scared of him."

Ah, but he had been, and I remembered what the third mate, Groff, had said about Harry's toting a gun in his back pocket and Harry in a nasty mood with a gun was nobody to cross. Also, as a deckhand, Buckley had the habit of obedience. But I wasn't Harry Loomis and Buckley had no fear of me.

"So you had to get it to me," I said, smoothing it over, "but you didn't have it when you got here. Maybe you left it someplace. Did you think of that? Of course you did. You're intelligent. You know how it is when a guy gets to drinking. You felt high and what-the-hell and you left it sitting on a bar when you walked out. I've done the same myself many times."

"That's what *you* say," he jeered. "How do I know what happened? I was soused. For all I know, you got it stashed under your mattress right this minute."

"Go and look."

"Oh no, Cap. You wouldn't be that dumb."

"Think back, Jeff. What bars did you go into that day?"

"All of them."

"On Market Street?"

"Any bar that came along. I was sick and tired of bay rum. I went in every gin mill from Port Newark on in. You think I was soused that day? You're nuts. Hell, I been so soused my face was swole up like a red balloon. And I been souseder'n that, too. It took half the cops in Tacoma to stick me in the clink and they hadda give me a needle on top of it. But I ain't never left nothing in no bars except maybe three-four guys stretched out on the floor." He laughed loudly and emptily. "Cousin, you don't know nothing about soused till you seen me when I get going!" His laugh blatted out again.

He wasn't crazy. Don't get that idea. He was in a high, odd state of elation with undertones of resentment and violence. He was simmering in alcohol and from one second to the next, it was a toss-up whether he'd pat you on the back or fracture your skull, and he was goaded by what seemed to him a conspiracy to keep him among the permanently poor. That I had been able to figure out, though much good it did me.

While I was trying to think of a way to keep him pacified, someone rapped four times on the hall door. Buckley was on his feet instantly with an agility and swiftness you'd never have thought possible in so big a man. He moved like a speedy lightweight and thank God I wasn't the over-imaginative type or I'd have found it pretty terrifying to think what it would be like if he really went for me. I'd have been a heap of bloody bones in a corner before I knew what happened to me.

He put a thick finger to his lips, tilted his chin at the door and darted into the bedroom. I went to answer the knock, praying for the first time that it would be Flavin and Gilman. Among the three of us, we could handle the big maniac and put him where he belonged for a while—in the psychiatric ward in City Hospital.

But it was about the worst person possible—Juan Garcia. My only thought was to get rid of him immediately but before I could close the door he was by me like an eel and stood in the middle of the living room, smilingly showing me a gun on the end of which was an odd bulbous contrivance. I'd never seen such a thing before but I knew it was a silencer.

"It is imperative that we have a conversation, *Señor* Malone," he said in that polite, liquid voice of his. "The *policia* are becoming increasingly active and unless we move quickly, your usefulness may be terminated suddenly. I am certain you will agree that such a misfortune would be exceedingly regrettable, both to you and to the gentleman I represent."

I said, "You're getting out of here," and started for him, certain he wouldn't shoot. He needed me alive, not dead.

I wasn't very bright that day. He didn't point the gun at my head or my middle but, still smiling, he lowered the silenced muzzle and aimed at my right thigh, cocking one eyebrow pleasantly—if an eyebrow could be cocked pleasantly under the circumstances.

"*Por favor, señor*. There is no need for an unpleasantness." He stepped back and waggled the gun at the sofa. "We will be seated and talk calmly. It is, as I have said, most necessary. There has been a waste of time too much already."

There was nothing I could do but let him talk and get it over. I did not want to be shot in the leg, even politely. I walked around him and sat on the sofa. He took the lounge chair with his back to the bedroom door, holding the gun ready in his lap.

"It is very possible, *Señor* Malone," he said, "that you do not have this thing that was in the possession of Harry Loomis. We know there was a messenger, one Jeff Buckley, a sailor. We know also that this Buckley was in a state of extreme intoxication on the day in question and visited several *cantinas* after leaving the *barco* with the package. You observe, we are most thorough in this. Much is at stake."

"Yeah," I said. "The whole future of your country, but please don't give me any more Fourth of July speeches."

He shrugged. "Very well, *señor*. We are men of experience and I admit this is a private venture. But that changes nothing, although you can see now that circumstances can be as hazardous for my principal as they are for you. Further, he is in the position of losing a large amount of money unless certain things are done."

"What things?"

He leaned forward and said earnestly, using the gun like a finger to emphasize his points, "As we analyze it, *Señor* Malone, this *borracho*, the sailor Buckley, may be the key to the matter. Did he, we ask ourselves, perhaps leave this package in one of the several *cantinas* he visited before coming here? It is, after the fashion of *borrachos*, quite possible, no? Unfortunately, the man has vanished. We cannot find him. This is unfortunate for we believe he could be persuaded to tell us of his perambulations on that day."

I was having trouble swallowing but could not help saying, "You mean you'll beat the hell out of him."

"If necessary, but that is of no consequence. The man is of the lowest type. Now, *señor*, we have reason to believe this animal will revisit you. We want him and you will turn him over to us. What happens to him later, as I have explained, is of no consequence. For this slight assistance, you will be paid the sum of five thousand dollars and—"

I wanted to yell at him to stop, to shut up, to run, but I didn't have the time. The bedroom door flung wide and Buckley was on Garcia before my mouth was half open to frame the words. He took Garcia's chin in his huge right hand and with one wrench folded the Latin's head over the back of the chair like a towel. There was a muted, sickening snap and Garcia went limp, the gun wilting from his hand.

Incredulous, I stared. "He's dead," I said stupidly.

Buckley laughed wildly. "They don't come deader,

Cap, I can bust anybody when I put my mind to it." Then, as if suddenly realizing the enormity of what he had done, he snarled, "And keep your yap shut, understand?" Gruesomely, he took the dead man by the collar, heaved him into my lap and ran from the apartment, laughing like a lunatic.

Flavin and Gilman gave me a going-over that must have been the quickest in police history. They and the body of Garcia were out of the apartment an hour after I called them. I told them everything—Buckley's conversation and Garcia's conversation—and they listened without comment. Even they could see that, strong as I was, I didn't have the tremendous muscle power to break a man's neck before he could fire a shot from the gun he was holding. In fact, it's almost impossible to break a man's neck if he resists.

"Put it on the wire," Flavin said tersely to Gilman, "Stress that Buckley's extremely dangerous and take no chances with him. I warned you, Malone, I told you the guy would go berserk some day. Why didn't you call us when you saw he had finally crossed the line?"

"And get my neck broken, too? He damn near pulled my arms off as it was."

"You could have figured a way."

"It happened too fast."

"All right, all right, I'm not going to argue with you, and if you think I believe any of this stuff you told me, you're crazy."

"I gave it to you just the way it happened."

"Nuts. What was the fight about—the split? Was Garcia trying to hold out on Buckley or what?"

"There was nothing to split," I said wearily. "I was—"

"Okay, have it your own way. You've had your chance to come clean with us and the hell with you. If Buckley doesn't get you after this, Garcia's pals will. See you in the morgue, sucker."

So in the end I sat there alone with the memory of Garcia's horribly limp neck as clear before me as if it were happening all over again. I shuddered. I remembered the other gun I had taken from the Latin the night before and went into the bedroom and got it from the pocket of my gray suit. It was a .38, a stubby, bad-tempered looking gun with a three-inch barrel. It felt cold in my hand and looked woefully inadequate.

The phone rang and the sound of it actually raised me off the floor, I was that jangled.

It was Claire and she said quickly, "I'm sorry about last night, Joe. I didn't mean any of those things I said to you. I was upset and scared and, oh, I don't know, things seemed to close in on me suddenly. I'm truly sorry I acted the way I did. You're the only friend I have here, truly you are, and if I hurt you with what I said, I apologize. Will you forgive me? Please?"

My heart lifted at the sound of her sweet, light clear voice, but in the very next moment it thudded down again. The happenings of the day, the way it had piled up so ominously, made it impossible for me to see her without endangering her, too. There was nothing I could do but stay away from her until this was over. I groaned, so much did I want to see her, but I couldn't, not without dragging her in with me.

"Forgive what?" I said, hardening my voice. "You were drunk. So what? Stay away from liquor if you can't hold it."

I heard her gasp. "But truly, Joe," she stammered, "I wasn't—"

"You were cockeyed, baby, and if there's anything I can't stand, it's a sloppy female drunk."

"Joe please, I—"

"Go home, sister. Go back to the farmers in Ohio. Stick to Sunday school picnics and ice cream festivals. You're up the wrong alley here."

She started to say more but I hung up and stared bleakly at the phone for several minutes.

It was a wonderful day, just wonderful.

Eleven

It was dusk and I sat in the gathering gloom. With Garcia dead, I no longer had a point of departure; but, if he had been telling the truth, he was only one of the hired hands anyway. Bunny Riordan was another and probably even less important. I was not going to search the city for Bunny. That would have been futile and I knew if I sat tight, somebody would come for me. Somebody had to come. The urgency was growing hour by hour and they had to come to me before the police did. So when the phone rang again, I sprang to answer it.

This time it was Janice Noonan and she said, "Oh, Joe!" Then, fervently, "Thank God!"

It hit me all in a bunch and I said heavily, "So you're part of it, too, Janice. That's why you gave me that invitation to the Esplanade last night. How dumb can I get!"

She made no attempt to deny or explain, but rushed on as if she had to get the words out before something happened. "Joe, listen to me, please. Get out of your apartment. You're in terrible danger. You don't know how terrible the danger is. They've heard about Mr. Garcia and they're furious. They're going to do something to you. Please Joe, go some place, hide, but don't stay there!"

"I'm not running, baby."

"Please, Joe, I beg you."

"Who are 'they,' Janice?"

"I—I can't tell you, Joe. Don't ask me, but I can't let them hurt you. I had to warn you. Go away. Please, please, please! Don't stay there."

"How much do you know about all this, Janice?"

"So little," she moaned, "so very little."

"What did they use you for, a decoy or something?"

"I don't know, Joe, I honestly don't know. But please don't waste time talking. Get out of your apartment right now! It's come to a head and they—they're going to do something, something bad. Listen to me, please. I wouldn't be talking to you like this unless it were urgent."

I thought quickly. I had a gun, but I wasn't the smartest guy in the world and what good would a showdown do me at this point? I still didn't know what it was all about and a shooting, if it came to that, wouldn't help me a bit. On the other hand, maybe they were using Janice to sucker me out into the open—though I didn't really believe that. She was head over heels in this mess and had deliberately lured me to the Esplanade House last night, but I didn't think she'd go along with cold-blooded violence or murder. She was still Janice Noonan, the kid I'd grown up with, if you know what I mean. I admit she was out after the dollar in the quickest and easiest way she knew, but I couldn't believe she had gone bad all the way.

And there was something else, too—she knew who 'they' were ...

"There's no place I can go, Janice," I said. "To the police, sure, but then you'll be dragged into it."

"No, not the police, Joe!"

"There you are. If I go to a hotel, it'd be only a few hours before they'd find out. Hotels will be the first places they'll check. I don't have any relatives around here, and I wouldn't get them mixed up in it even if I did. So where can I go? I have to stay here."

She was too distracted to see the flaws. "No, no, no, Joe. You *can't* stay there. Listen. Come to my apartment. You can hide here for a day or so anyway—they'll never think of looking here—and maybe we can think of a place to hide you. You have to hide, Joe! You're in worse danger than anything you can imagine. They'll have no mercy. They think you and—and Harry Loomis planned to double-cross them right from the beginning. They might even—kill you!"

My God, I thought, she must have turned pretty bad if, knowing that, she still won't name names. On the other hand, they might have terrorized her so thoroughly that she was incapable of going further.

Still, she had asked me to come to her apartment and that was what I wanted. I'd have gone anyway, but it was a thousand times better this way. It put us in this thing together and if I managed right, there was a chance she might talk. Damn it, she had risked warning me, so there could be a way of getting more of a response from her.

"I'll be over as fast as I can, Janice," I told her.

"Come in the basement door at the side, Joe. I'll unlock it for you."

I couldn't just walk out of my apartment, get in my car and drive to her apartment in Forest Hill, the expensive section of Newark. The car and the doors would be watched. I went down to the cellar and crawled through the small window at the end which let out into a scraggly stand of leafy rhododendron. This joined an overgrown box hedge next door and by wriggling through the shrubbery I was able to get almost a block from the apartment without going out into the open street. Then I walked. It was a long way, but I couldn't risk a lighted bus or a cab. The basement door of her apartment house was open for me and I climbed the stairs to the second floor before taking the elevator to her apartment on the top floor, the one with the five hundred-dollar-a-month view of Branch Brook Park.

She was waiting for me and you'd never have recognized her as the vital, glamorous girl of last night. She was wearing no make-up and the unnatural pallor of her face made her look ill. Even her black hair seemed to have lost some of its lustre. She had on a dark green quilted nylon housecoat, which she alternately opened a little at the neck or hugged to her as if she had chills and fever. There was nothing under the housecoat but she was too upset to realize it.

"Thank God!" was the first thing she said. And then, "I just called the club. I told them I was sick. I can't go on tonight. If I tried to sing, I think I'd scream. Do you want a drink? I'm afraid to take one myself. I've got some of those tranquilizing pills but I'm afraid to take them, too. If I put anything in my stomach I *would* be sick. Look—" she held out her pale, trembling hands. "This is the most horrible thing, Joe. But I didn't mean what I said. About their killing you. I was hysterical. They wouldn't go that far."

"What do you think happened to Harry Loomis?" I asked bluntly.

"He—he was killed in a fight," she faltered. "With that sailor who killed Mr. Garcia."

"Jeff Buckley has a gilt-edged alibi for the Loomis murder. Your friends killed Harry. Why kid yourself, Janice?"

"I don't believe it!"

"Garcia admitted it to me."

"I don't believe it!" she cried, covering her ears with her hands. "They wouldn't go that far. I know they wouldn't, so stop saying it. Stop it, stop it!"

I stopped. She didn't want to face it and if I tried to force her, there was every chance her mind wouldn't take it. She was too close as it was. She'd go clean off if I pushed too hard.

"Do you know what you're mixed up in, Janice?" I asked quietly, soothing her.

She shook her head. "I wish I did, Joe. I wish to God I did. You don't know how awful it is, not knowing."

"Harry was carrying something for them. Where did he get it? At the Panama Canal?"

"I don't know, I don't know, I don't know!" Then, with an effort, she fought back to a semblance of calm. "I made two trips to South America for them."

I could barely conceal a surge of elation. She did want to get clear of this thing or she wouldn't have told me that much—and, without realizing it, she had told me much more. She knew some names but without the rest of it, the names didn't mean anything and just speaking the names without anything to back it up, she herself would be in danger, and that's what terrified her.

"What did you do in South America?" I asked.

"That's just it," she said dully. "I didn't do anything."

"Didn't you see anybody? Didn't someone contact you there?"

"No. I just travelled through. The first time it was Ecuador and Colombia and the next time it was Colombia and Venezuela. I was just a tourist, that's all."

"Maybe you took something down with you. Or brought something back."

"Not without knowing it, Joe!"

"It could have been hidden in your luggage."

"I packed the bags myself. And unpacked them. There was nothing except my own things."

"I hate to sound like a B movie," I said in the same lulling voice, "but maybe there was a false bottom or something. Do you want to get out of this mess if you can, Janice?"

She bowed her head and after a long, agonized silence said in a scarcely audible voice, "I'm scared, Joe. I've never been so scared in my life. If I told what I know, it wouldn't be enough and they'd—do things to me."

"All right then. Maybe we can work it out. Let me see the luggage if you still have it."

"You can see it but it won't do any good," she said hopelessly. "It's just ordinary airplane luggage."

She got up from the sofa and walked heavily into the bedroom. She looked and moved as if she were twice her age and ill. She returned with two pieces of light gray luggage plastered thickly with the usual steamship and airline stickers. I put them on the floor and, kneeling, felt over every inch of them, inside and out. I didn't know a thing about false bottoms or secret compartments, but I did know this much—if there were such things in this luggage there would have been an extra thickness on the sides or bottom or top and I would have found it. An extra compartment wouldn't have fooled anybody who was really looking for it.

There was nothing. It was, as she said, ordinary, undoctored luggage, and I rocked back and squatted on my heels, frustrated. There had to be something. I knew it. They hadn't sent her to South America just for the ride. I stared at the two bags. At such moments your mind either goes completely blank or your perceptions are heightened. Mine must have heightened because I found myself staring at those veritable mats of travel stickers. There weren't just a few. The lids of both bags were thick with them. There were, in fact, too many. She'd have to have travelled for years to collect that many and the bags were practically new. My fingers beginning to shake, I reached out and worked one corner loose with my fingernail and the whole batch of stickers began to come up in a single sheet. They were not glued down in the usual way but had been stuck to the bag with rubber cement which, though it would hold firmly, could be more easily removed. There was my secret compartment, under the stickers!

That was as far as I got for, just as I was uttering an exclamation of triumph, something struck me heavily on the nape of the neck and a wave of blackness engulfed me.

When I opened my eyes, I was still in the same place on the floor but flat on my face and able to move only sluggishly. Janice, either unconscious or dead, was lying on the sofa, the housecoat stripped from her. Bunny Riordan stood grinning down at both of us and standing off to one side was the gaunt man who had told me about the fake telephone call in the Esplanade House the night before. He was holding a blue-black .45 and it looked the size of a trench mortar in his skinny hand. Bunny was slapping a spring-handled blackjack against the side of his leg.

"Well, well," he said when I rolled my head, "he came back to the land of the living."

He bent over and rapped me casually on the temple with the blackjack, not so hard as to knock me out again but enough to paralyze me. The gaunt man became a wavering silhouette against the light blue satin of the window drapes. Bunny ran his hand lightly up and down Janice's bare back.

"The skin you love to touch," he grinned. "Too bad she went sour on us. I hate to ruin a piece of high class goods like that. I'll show you what I mean."

And, winking at me as if it were a highly amusing joke, he beat her with the blackjack—head, shoulders, back and legs. I groaned and made a terrific effort to move and he laughed.

"Relax, old pal," he said. "She's out cold. She can't feel a thing." He struck her again on the head, a full-arm swing. "See? But she was a bad girl and I have to give her a spanking. She'll never do it again now, will she? You, though, that's something different. It's a shame but we'll have to get really rough with you."

He picked up something from the lamp table at the end of the sofa. It looked like a whip but the sweat came out of me when I saw what it really was. It was one of the specialties his sadistic mind had thought up—a twenty inch length of barbed wire stapled to a handle made from a broomstick. He laughed and swung it through the air, cocking his head as if enjoying the vicious whistling sound it made. Then, taking his time, he told me in foul detail exactly how he was going to work on me with it.

"On the other hand, old pal," he said, "I might go easy on you if you tell us where we can find that chump Buckley. Not that it would let you off entirely, Joe old pal—you've had this coming for a long time—but I might not drag it out for so long. Don't be in a hurry to talk, though. I need the exercise."

Another tap from the blackjack sent me into semi-consciousness and I felt him pull the coat from me. I thought I was seeing things when Jeff Buckley came through the window drapes like a wild-eyed apparition and sent the gaunt man flying at us with a crushing swing of his Herculean arm. It wasn't real, nothing was real in this phantasmagoria—his springing at Bunny and Bunny's quick flick across the eyes with the barbed wire whip, Buckley's stumbling back, bloody and blinded, roaring, Bunny's gliding in, the bright gleam of the knife blade in his hand turning red as he thrust and thrust and thrust again. Half-whimpering, half giggling, I got the gun from my pocket and, steadying it dreamily with both hands, shot Bunny in the chest. He straightened up, put one hand to his chest like a lawyer about to make a heart-felt plea to a jury, then, looking thoughtful, fell across Buckley.

I looked around me, bemused. There were four of them, none moving. Buckley, Bunny and the gaunt man on the floor and Janice Noonan nude and still on the sofa. I knew there was something I should do but couldn't think what. It occurred to me that if perhaps I washed my face with cold water, it might wake me up. I wavered to my hands and knees and crawled across the room, very carefully circling the crumpled figure of the gaunt man. If I touched him he might awaken, and he looked so peaceful, curled up there on the rug.

My next real recollection was that of being sick in the bathroom. Though still dizzy my head cleared sufficiently for me to walk back to the living room and

I was nearly sick all over again at what I saw. This time it was very real. Buckley was the only one who was even partially conscious and as I bent over him, his eye gleamed momentarily and he whispered something I could barely hear.

"I foxed you, Cap. Knew you'd come out. Followed you over here. Thought you locked me out. Foxed you again. Climbed the ledge around the outside of the building to window. I sure busted them guys, didn't I?"

"Yes, you busted them, Jeff."

His grin flickered faintly. "I c'n … bust anybody …" He sighed wearily and his eyes closed.

Janice's skull was splintered and she was dead. The gaunt man was dead, his neck broken like Garcia's. Bunny breathed, but there was a bloody froth at his mouth. My stomach coiled and clenched and I walked stiffly to the telephone and dialed "O" for Operator.

I gave her Janice's address, spelling it out carefully. "Call the police," I said. "There are dead people here."

I hung up and wiped the handset with my handkerchief and as I left I also wiped the doorknobs, inside and out. I went from the building by way of the basement. It took me over half an hour to reach my apartment, for again I dared not use a bus or cab.

I knew what was coming, and when Flavin and Gilman arrived, I was in my pajamas, my hair tousled as if I had just gotten up from bed. Flavin's glance was icy. "I suppose you've been here all the time," he said.

"All what time? I've been in bed." But even as I was speaking, a chilling thought came to me—my bed was as smoothly made as when I left it that morning and they had merely to glance in to know I was lying.

But Flavin folded his lips tightly. "I just came from your girl friend's apartment," he said. "Three dead, one dying. And there was no gun for the one who was shot. Somebody walked out of that place and I have a feeling it was you. How about it?"

"Janice Noonan?" It was no effort for me to look

sick.

"That's right. And your buck-toothed friend was there too, the one you called Bunny Riordan. He seems to have been up to something pretty nasty with a blackjack, a knife and a piece of barbed wire. Fingerprints told us that much. Now listen to me," he said harshly. "This is self-defense, pure and simple, and if you shot Riordan, you're in the clear. Do you understand? I'm giving you a chance to come clean, you stupid bastard!"

I knew that much. There'd be no murder charge but they could tie me up as a material witness. There was a slow-burning fury in me now and all I wanted was to get my hands on the cold-blooded devil behind all this.

"I've nothing to come clean about," I said tonelessly.

"Right!" he snapped. "That's just about what I expected from you. But get this—if Riordan lives long enough to breathe your name just once, Malone, I'm nailing you to the cross, so help me God! Let's go, Gilman."

Gilman paused briefly at the door to give me a glance in which there was contempt, a smoldering promise and an additional dark touch like death.

But was it any wonder that I thought of death?

Twelve

There were things on my mind. Janice Noonan. A few brief months ago I had been in a rage because she brushed me off for that City Hall leech, Jack Garrity. Now she was dead. Instead of poignant grief, all I felt was a numbed melancholy, remembering her not in the height of her beauty but her fresh quickness in the days when we were growing up together on the streets of the Ironbound. There was also the slow fury, though the reasons for that were complex and Janice was but part of the pattern.

And in a way I was sorry for big Jeff Buckley, too, a man driven to excesses by impotent rages. He had in effect rejected us, his people, but it was shameful all the same that he should die at the hand of one like Bunny Riordan. There, too, was Harry Loomis, possibly a useless and violent man, dead because of his greed, but in the end he had had his one decent, if somewhat cloudy, impulse when he thought finally to provide for an almost-forgotten daughter.

Yes, and that brought me to Claire—but I did not want to think of Claire.... As if called up by the very thoughts of her that flooded me, the bell rang and her voice came through the thin panel of the door, speaking my name, pleading. I sat perfectly still, staring bleakly at a spot on the rug six feet in front of me. She rang again and then knocked, calling several times. At length there was silence and when I looked up I saw the white oblong of an envelope beneath the door. It was a long while before I crossed the room and picked it up. It was not sealed and I turned it stiffly in my hands as if my fingers were knotted with arthritis, but I did not read it. I took it to the coffee table, on which the thin incisions from Buckley's knife were plainly visible, tore it into small pieces and burned it in the large metal ashtray. It was not an easy thing to do, and while the flaking gray ash still glowed I took it quickly to the kitchen and emptied it out the window.

I returned to the living room and sat down doggedly to think. I had never been a thinker and it came hard. I didn't know where to start. A hard day's work is no substitute for it and for too long I had done all my thinking with my muscles or my fists or had drunk my way out of the necessity. Now I had to think and I didn't know how to go about it.

All right, start with Janice, I told myself stubbornly. She had been sent to South America. Why? I had no answer until I happened to remember her luggage and the way the travel stickers had been plastered on with rubber cement. So she had carried something down or brought something back, but what could be concealed in so thin a space? A paper? That was silly. A paper could be mailed with perfect safety. But wait. There was something else. *She* hadn't brought anything back. It was Harry Loomis who had done that. She had taken something down and someone had lifted it from her luggage during her stay. But what and why? I was doing fine. A bright ten-year-old in the sixth grade couldn't have done better. I had no more idea of what and why than I did of the worlds outside the solar system, but though I may not have been smart, I was obstinate. I stuck with it.

All right, then—who? I asked myself. The obvious choice there was Garcia, the Spanish-speaking Latin. If there had been business to conduct in South America, he would have been the one. He had been outside the law up here, so he probably had been the same down there, which meant his presence there had to be innocent-seeming and there was something he had been afraid to have found on him when he went into South America. That was where Janice had been employed. She had taken that something to him.

Now all this took a lot more time to puzzle out than it does to tell. For each morsel of fact I extracted, I had to wade through a ton of sludge. The next step should have been easy, but my brains were honestly aching before I came up with an answer.

If Harry Loomis brought something back, what did Janice take down to Garcia? Money—an amount of money which would have been suspicious had the police found it on him when he entered the country. Janice had gone once to Ecuador and Venezuela but twice to Colombia. I didn't have to be a genius to decide Garcia's stamping ground was Colombia, and he was the purchasing agent.

But what had he bought in Colombia? Not drugs. If they were dealing in drugs, Mexico was closer and safer and a much bigger drug producer. What *could* you buy in Colombia anyway? Panama hats? Straw sandals? Indian blankets? This was all ridiculous, but when you're out of the habit, your mind flies off in all directions and what did I know about Colombia in the first place? District of Columbia. Columbia The Gem Of The Ocean. But the South American Colombia could have been the capital of Bongo Bongo, for all I knew.

Then I had the first inspiration of my entire life. Bivens, the janitor, had three kids, and people with kids sometimes had encyclopedias and, as I remembered encyclopedias, they could tell you more about anything than you wanted to know.

I put on my flannel robe and a pair of slippers and went down to his basement apartment. He did not have a set of encyclopedias. Encyclopedias cost money, he explained. Would a dictionary do? He had a dictionary around some place maybe, though he didn't think so. Kids nowadays, all they wanted was comic books and TV, but just so long as they did their homework, well, you know how kids are.

I didn't and I don't think he did either because his oldest, aged ten, who had been standing there taking it all in, made the only intelligent suggestion in the entire conversation.

"We got the Book of Knowledge, papa."

"We do?"

"Yeah, mama got it with box tops and fifty cents, remember? It's like an encyclopedia, Mr. Malone, not a whole set, just one book."

"Does it tell you about the different countries in South America?" I asked eagerly.

"Oh sure. All kinds of things. I'll show you...."

Three minutes later I was hurrying back to my apartment, clasping the cheap, gaudily-covered book as if it were a certified check for a million dollars. I couldn't wait to get it open. The paper was tissue-thin and the print tiny and blurred, as if the plates had been on the press since Gutenberg, but there was a map and a page and a half all about Colombia. I read it so hurriedly the first time, it didn't mean a thing. The second time wasn't much better—it had an area of 439,828 square miles, a population of 11,260,000 and the capitol was Bogotá. Then there was a lot more geography and a lot of history and a whole mess of Spanish-looking names of people and places, all ending in *o* or *a*. I went through it five times, reading that fine print until my eyes watered, and then I hit it. There were only two lines but when I found them, they seemed to stand out as big and black as a *Daily News* headline.

"Colombia is known for its fine emeralds. This is a government monopoly and the gems are exported only under rigid supervision."

Emeralds! Why, a good emerald was as valuable as diamond! And thieves' markets operated the same everywhere. Stolen or smuggled gems could be bought by fence for a fraction of the real value. With twenty thousand dollars, say, you could buy yourself a fortune in illicitly-obtained stones. And with the market controlled by the Colombians, there was bound to be stealing and smuggling and maybe even crooked officials with itchy fingers. Was there such a thing as a politician *without* itchy fingers?

And Janice had made two trips, and undoubtedly others had made trips before her. They had a system and were cashing in. God knows how much Loomis had gotten away with in that last bundle. No wonder murder was only a detail in this operation. Men gambled their lives to take a few thousand dollars from a bank, and here was a wealth to make any crook's mouth water. Murder? Murder was nothing in a deal of this size. Even a massacre wouldn't have been anything, with that much at stake.

That made me swallow hard and feel the sick coiling of my stomach again. There *had* been a massacre, practically. And who'd be next? How *many* would be next? Me and how many others? Me and who else might get in their way? Me and—

I stopped right there. There was nothing for me in that kind of thinking except the gibbering meemees. I bent over the Book of Knowledge again. Oh, sweet Book of Knowledge! When this was all over I was going to buy myself the biggest Book of Knowledge in the metropolitan area and have it stuffed and mounted and hung over the fireplace like a prized trophy and if some day I had kids, I'd read them a chapter every night, like the Old Testament and—

Stop it! Stop gibbering!

But I wasn't gibbering. My mind was just gathering itself again and it began to focus and function when I bent over the pink, yellow and blue half-page map of Colombia, to which was attached the twisting umbilical of Central America. It was the strangest damn thing, but now that I'd gotten a pattern of thinking—after all those skimmed years—the moment I laid eyes on the map I saw exactly how they had solved the problem of getting the emeralds out of the country, which, with the trade so rigidly controlled, would have been one of the booby traps for less organized thieves.

Remember, I had been an oiler in the black gang for the Inter-Coastal Line for awhile, and I'd made four trips through the Canal myself. Without that background, I wouldn't have seen it so quickly, if at all.

You see, a boat never goes straight through the Canal, the way it might go up a river or through a strait. There are always other boats and you have to anchor outside Colon on the Atlantic side or Balboa at the southern end while waiting your turn. And while you're sitting there waiting, natives come out in canoes and sell you trinkets or souvenirs or a bigger supply boat comes out with other things. (Remember Jeff Buckley's telling me the deck crew had bought a case of bay rum at the Canal?)

The Pacific Ocean Coast of Colombia is only a hundred and fifty miles across the *Golfo de Panama* from Balboa, where Harry Loomis' boat would have to anchor, after coming down from Washington State. That hundred and fifty miles would be an easy trip for a small fishing boat, an inconspicuous, anonymous boat, on which a package of emeralds could be carried. Near the anchorage, the gems could be transferred to a fake native canoe. Garcia himself, unshaven and ragged, could pass as a half-breed—and who would there be to get suspicious if the mate of a freighter "bought" a souvenir of Panama from a screeching, gesticulating native? Nobody. And who'd know emeralds had been passed in the patently innocent pur-chase? It was practically foolproof. Furthermore, coastal freighters which don't put in at foreign ports are not subject to customs inspection. Harry could walk down the gangplank at Port Newark, tossing the gems in his hand and there wouldn't be a soul around to question if they were pebbles or glass.

It wasn't as easy as all that, mind you—the Colombian coast guard could knock off the fishing boat or Garcia could have gotten nabbed while buying the stones—but I couldn't think of an easier way to get them into this country, or out of Colombia, or a less suspicious way to transfer them to Harry.

And it was at this point my mind stopped working intelligently. I was exulting and gloating and so full of myself that you'd have thought I'd just cracked the top secret Russian military code. I didn't stop to realize this wasn't the whole answer. I called Flavin at Headquarters.

"I just figured out what Harry Loomis had in that package," I said. "Emeralds."

"Do you have them?"

"Let me expl—"

"Do you know who does have them?"

"No, but—"

He said disgustedly, "Ah, for crissake. I'm getting sicker of you by the minute!"

I stared stupidly at the phone, hardly able to believe he had hung up before I could tell him how smart I had been.

Then the reaction set in. What did I really have? Nothing, not a damn thing. Jeff Buckley said he tried to get the package to me. "I had to get it to you, see? I *had* to." His exact words. But he hadn't gotten it to me. Loomis and Garcia knew about the stones, but they were dead. So there was nothing, actually, I could have told Flavin. I didn't blame him for hanging up on me.

And maybe the whole idea about emeralds and smuggling and all the rest of the kit and kaboodle was cockeyed, too. I had no tangible facts, only a theory. And the Book of Knowledge. The good old Book of Knowledge. "Colombia is known for its fine emeralds. This is a government monopoly and the gems are exported only under rigid supervision."

Wonderful.

South Africa was known for its fine diamonds and

in Switzerland you could buy cuckoo clocks and if you went to Havana they gave you free drinks in the rum factories.

Have a drink, Malone. You've earned it. Have a mickey on the rocks. I tramped morosely into the kitchen and poured myself a double shot of rye. It went down with as much jolt as a glass of water. In my state, they could have given me a beaker of old time popskull, aged in the barrel with a handful of gunpowder and a rattlesnake head, and it wouldn't have made me blink. I had another.

It knocked me cold.

Thirteen

I woke up on the sofa with the sun hot and clenching on my face and in the corner the phone was a shrilling little black monster, furiously demanding attention. I didn't have a hangover but I felt dull and sodden, the way you do after passing out on too little liquor after an exhausting day. I hoped if I turned over and closed my eyes the phone would stop, but it didn't, and finally I labored to my feet, trudged the long mile across the room and mumbled a hello into the handset.

A voice said sharply, "Malone?" and I said, "What is it?" and it said, "Hold on."

The next instant I was fully awake and gripping the phone until my knuckles stood out white and pointed. It was Claire and she was crying, "Don't listen to them, Joe. Don't—" Her voice was cut off abruptly, as if by muffling hand, and I heard a scuffle of feet as she was pulled away.

The first person—it was a man but he was speaking through a piece of cloth or something—came back again. "Did you recognize that voice, Malone?"

"What do you want?" I asked thickly.

"Go to Branch Brook Park. Take a slow walk south, starting at the tennis courts. We'll pick you up."

"Wait a minute," I said desperately trying to think of something to say, something to delay. "You're not giving me enough time."

"Time for what?"

"To—get what you want—me to give you. I don't have it here."

"Somebody'll go with you to get it, then."

I groaned. This was the final edge and I couldn't take a step in any direction. "It—it won't work that way—" I stammered.

"Why not?"

"I've—got it set up so I have to go after the package

alone. You don't think Harry and I were the only ones in this, do you? There's another guy and if somebody else shows up with me—damn it, he's got a gun and he'll use it!" I shouted.

"You're stalling, Malone."

"Use your head, you dumb bastard!" I cried, trying to keep a half thought ahead of my words. "Harry and I couldn't swing this ourselves and if you had any brains you'd know it."

"Know what?"

I couldn't go on improvising forever. He was pressing me too closely and too fast.

"Emeralds!" I blurted. "If you want me to come right out with it, all right. Emeralds, emeralds, emeralds!"

That was a prayer, believe me, but it worked and he snapped, "Shut up! Are you slugnutty? Shove a glove in your mouth if you can't keep it closed. They rung the bell on you. Shut up!"

An almost forgotten bit of thanksgiving went up from me and I was able to say, "You wouldn't believe me so I told you."

"So you told me, stumblebum, now shut up for a minute!" Maybe he needed to calm down a little himself. "All right, sonny. It's ten o'clock. I'll give you till noon, then you take that walk through the park like I told you."

"One o'clock," I said. "It'll take me an hour and a half each way, at the very least."

I could feel his silence like a tightening fist. "You're shifty, Malone. You're fast on your feet. Always were. But this ain't the time for it, understand. None of your sneak punches, see? No cops, no tricks. We've got the girl, mind?"

"Yes. No tricks."

"And the more you stall, the less of the girl you'll get back. You mind that, too?"

"I'm not stalling. I'll be in the park at one o'clock."

"Don't forget, sonny, you'll be watched before you're picked up. That's one thing, and the other is this—just to make absolutely sure, we're not turning the girl loose till twenty-four hours after you give us what's rightfully ours. You're on the ropes, Malone, and there's nothing you can do, unless you want us to send you the girl piece by piece afterwards. You got till one o'clock and that's all."

I didn't hear the rattle of his phone when he hung up. I couldn't have heard anything. I was drenched with perspiration. My pajamas were soaked. It ran into my eyes and my mouth and was salty on my tongue. It was ten o'clock. In three hours it would be one o'clock, and from one o'clock on it would be all over but the final horrors. What could I do in a hundred and eighty minutes? Where could I go that I hadn't been already? Who could I see? What could I say? Even if I could have expected help from Flavin, I didn't dare go to him.

Suddenly I could hear my two-dollar alarm clock as if it were a tom-tom beating in the bedroom, and each beat another fragment of time wasted. My first thought was to get dressed and I dashed into the other room, peeling off my pajamas as I ran. I jumped in and out of the shower to wash the sweat off me, shaved in thirty seconds and then dressed.

I put on my new gray suit, a fresh white shirt, my best Black Watch tartan woolen tie, a pair of dark Argyle socks I'd never worn and the twenty-dollar scotch-grain shoes I saved for special occasions. This was very important, you understand. I had to look my absolute best. Don't ask me why, but this was a serious matter, and right then I would no more have gone out in slacks and a sport jacket than I would have appeared in public in my underwear. Even my hair had to be combed with that greaseless pomade so it wouldn't get mussed. Maybe you think it ridiculous but it wasn't to me. It was extremely important. I didn't waste time primping, you realize, but I had to put on the best of everything I had.

And when the rush and urgency of getting dressed was over, I was left standing in front of the mirror, staring at a blank face without a single idea behind it. There I was, all dressed up and no place to go, only this time it wasn't a joke. If only that voice on the phone had meant something to me, but it had been so muffled by whatever he put over the mouthpiece that it had no more identity than a whisper or a shriek. I couldn't work on that.

Inescapably, there was only one thing I could do and to face it meant an almost certain admission of defeat—I had to find the package. In three hours. All along I'd been saying Buckley had left it in a gin mill, but there are a thousand gin mills in the Newark area, and he had ranged as far south as Rahway. Also, in that whisky-blackout he went into, he could have left it almost anywhere—in a bus, on a park bench, in the men's room at Penn Station, in a phone booth; he could have dropped it on the street or in a cigar store. I could go on forever that way, and he had roamed a space of almost a hundred square miles in an alcoholic fog.

He said he *had* to get the package to me, repeated it and emphasized it, and that much I believed. Harry Loomis was the one person of whom he had been afraid and he knew if he fluffed the errand, he'd be in for it. In a nasty mood, and this would have been a real blow-off, Harry was bad—and he was carrying a gun. Yes, Buckley would have been anxious to get the package to me and he would have done everything possible, but with a rummy like that, they don't realize the drinks are affecting them and it's let's-have-just-one-more and half a block away is another gin mill.

I knew I had to make a try or at the end of three hours I'd still be staring at my dumb Irish face in the mirror, so I picked the gin mills. They were the most logical. You walk into a gin mill, you have a package, you put it on the bar, you have a few drinks, you walk out and maybe the package comes with you and maybe it doesn't. I went over Buckley's probable itinerary in my mind. The bus from Port Newark would land him in Penn Station and from there he could have taken another bus straight to my place, but he hadn't taken the second bus. He wanted a drink. On Market Street from Penn Station west for six blocks on both sides of the street was the thickest concentration of taverns in the city, and down near the Station were the tough rumdum hangouts. They got better as you walked west, but the majority of the bartenders were hard-bitten characters who'd seen everything, believed nothing and gave nothing. If Buckley himself walked in and asked for the package, they'd given it to him if they had it. A barkeep might knock down on the till every chance he gets, but he's usually pretty honest in other ways. Too, through long experience, they've trained themselves to remember people and Buckley, with his height and brute bulk, was certainly memorable. Now if I walked in and asked for the package, I'd get a cynical shrug and "You got the wrong place, bud. Nobody left a package here," and you can't blame them. Why should they give Buckley's package to a stranger?

Just when I was beginning to go round and round again, I remembered Alec Curry and his saying to come to him if necessary. My spirits lifted because he really could do something. Everybody knew Alec Curry—in the gin mill circuit, that is. Not that he was much of a drinker, but all kinds of characters, including bartenders, used his gym for a hangout, promoting bets, making contacts or just watching the fighters work. And he always had a dozen stooges who did odd jobs for coffee and doughnuts, and if he gave each one of them a note, they could help me canvass the taverns, and he might even go out with me himself. It was a long shot, I knew, but sometimes the long shots paid off, and I felt a hundred per cent better.

I drove my car downtown and, sure enough, a dark blue sedan drifted along behind me. Flavin had me covered. I left the car in a parking lot, walked to my bank on Broad Street and drew out two hundred dollars. I'd get more freely-given help from Alec Curry if it didn't cost him money. Then I walked up Bank Street to Bamberger's Department Store. There were two detectives with me. I had them spotted. The one ahead of me had on a brown suit and the one in back a blue suit. I lost one of them at the close-out dress sale in the crowded basement, and the other by being the last one into a jam-packed elevator on the main floor. I saw him turn and run for the escalator as the elevator doors closed. I got off at the second floor and, taking no chances, sprinted down the west stairs and left the building by way of the loading platforms on Washington Street. With pure luck, I got a cruising cab at the corner and rode down to Mulberry Street, a half-block from Alec Curry's gym.

There my luck ended abruptly. The gym was on the second floor of an old red brick building and nailed to the street-level entrance was a sign, *Closed For Repairs*. I reached out mechanically and tried the door and it was really locked. But it couldn't be. It was one of those practical jokes, like the hot-foot or limburger behind the sweatband of your hat, the regulars at the gym were always playing on each other, and when I turned away somebody would stick his head out and give me the haw-haw horse laugh. My hand half-lifted to try the knob again but by this time I knew it wasn't a joke and the gym was really closed for repairs, though God knows it would have taken an earthquake and the San Francisco fire to force Alec Curry to close shop when there was good money to be made.

A heavy-muscled, knot-eared man in an old sweatshirt and khaki work pants, leaning against the building beside the door, said in an amiable but mushy voice, "It's closed, mister."

I didn't recognize him but I knew what he was—an ex-fighter who'd been in there too long and had taken more than his quota of hammering. A punchy. Not one of the bad ones—he didn't twitch—but a punchy all the same.

"Where can I find Alec Curry?" I asked.

"Tuesday," he said.

"What?"

"Tuesday. The plumbing, it's a flood. Tuesday it opens."

"But where's Alec? I want to talk to him."

"Alec? Ah, yeah. His brother."

It took me a minute. "He's visiting his brother? Where?"

"No. He'll be back Tuesday. It opens Tuesday."

"But what about his brother? Is he staying with his brother?"

That was a little too much for him. "Down the shore?" he said doubtfully.

"His brother lives at the shore?"

He brightened. "'Lantic City," he said happily.

That was the end of that and I said, "Thanks," turning away. Atlantic City was a hundred and twenty-five miles south, at least four hours in time on the busy highway. No matter where I stepped, the earth fell away from under my feet. My fists bunched but it was impotent anger—there was nothing to hit.

I kept moving. I had to. Two blocks down was the Essex Bar & Grill, a big, cheap-drink joint, but I knew the bartender. It was as good a place as any to start. I went there. The barkeep's name was Frank and he greeted me like an old friend, though I hadn't been in for months.

"Ah, Malone," he said noisily, "you shanty Irish son of a bitch. I thought you was dead or wounded. Rye on the rocks with a beer chaser?"

"No drinks this time, Frank," I said. "Business. A couple days ago you had a customer, a big guy, six feet four or five, blond and probably soused. He had a package but he lost it. Did he leave it here?" His face remained the same, his professional grin was still there, but a shutter closed in his eyes and I was an outsider, click, just like that.

"We get a lot of customers, Malone," he said. "I'd go nuts if I tried to keep track of them." I understood. He didn't have to hang out a sign. "The cops've been here, eh?"

He started to say something else but changed his mind and said flatly, "They've been. And I'm to report if anybody comes asking. The only thing you asked for was a drink, wasn't it?"

"Rye on the rocks but no beer chaser," I said.

He nodded as if it were an ordinary order and went down the bar. Any other barman and I'd have had the cops all over me like dandruff. The drink looked like rye on the rocks when he brought it, but it was pure ginger ale. He took my four bits and gave me two quarters in change.

"Keep moving," he said, and walked away.

It was the best advice he could have given me, but what could I do with it? I took two sips of the ginger ale and got out, but the dusty sunshine and undigested gas fumes from the scurrying traffic was no improvement. It had been one discouraging thing after another—Alec Curry's gym being closed and now the slap-in-the-face news that the police had already combed the gin mills, though if I'd had any sense I'd have known that. Flavin was a smart cop and he wasn't missing a thing—except the obvious. Obvious to me, that is.

But you know, when things pile up, you reach a point at which it can't get worse and either you throw up your hands and go down for the third time or you get stubbornly mad. I was red Irish and I got mad. It was the kind of senseless rage in which you stand out in the open and shake your fists at the sky and swear. It might not do any good but it was a hell of a lot better than blowing your brains out. I didn't shake my fists, but I swore. And it did do some good. It made me realize I was wasting time and being a damn fool. I hadn't had any breakfast and I need a place to sit down and think, so I walked up the street to the Waldorf Cafeteria and had a cup of coffee and a jelly doughnut. Though I drank only half of the coffee and didn't eat the doughnut, I did come up with an idea, which for me was practically a stroke of genius. It was something Flavin and Gilman had said. They'd been needling me, not giving out information, but it was one of those funny-looking little pieces of jigsaw you can't find a place for till the puzzle is almost all put together. Who's paying her rent these days, Sergeant, Flavin had said, Stocker the jeweler?

Ah, but it fitted—it fitted beautifully. Emeralds, a crooked outfit, a jeweler. One of the toughest things in a jewel theft is getting rid of the stones, getting somebody to buy them at a decent price, and what better outlet could they ask than the most highly respected old-line jeweler in the county? Stocker tied in with Janice and he tied in with the gems. I paid my quarter at the door, looked up and down the street to make sure my police friends hadn't picked me up again, then grabbed the first cab and went to Stocker's place of business on south Broad Street.

It had no relation whatever with the installment-plan jewelers farther north. His store was in an old-fashioned brown front building and had two small square show windows. In one was a string of pearls on a dark burgundy fold of velvet and in the other a single diamond earring on a cube of polished ebony. And his business sign itself was almost invisible. On the brownstone wall beside the entrance door was a quiet brass plate on which the raised letters spelled out,

Stocker, Established 1887. If the installment-plan jewelers in the heart of the shopping district didn't have a neon mobile fifteen feet high in two colors, they were practically out of business. The inside of Stocker's place was as softly and tastefully lighted as a funeral home and had the same slightly dusty, slightly floral odor. In the center of the floor was a large, low round teakwood table on which stood a bone china vase of long-stemmed roses, the showiest piece in the whole store. Standing seemingly at random on the gray pebble-twist rug were three mahogany Sheraton tables, each with two facing chairs. There were no showcases or shelves or signs and nothing, in fact, on the mahogany paneled walls but a few etchings which looked as if they had been drawn by one of those old-time draftsmen like maybe Rembrandt. The lone salesman was very elegant in striped gray pants and a black jacket, but he too smelled faintly of dust and flowers. He didn't say anything but merely smiled as he rose from one of the tables and strolled leisurely toward me. It was that kind of place.

"I want to talk to Mr. Stocker," I said.

He looked politely regretful, as if he hated to be impolite but no one saw Mr. Stocker but God and I wasn't even Saint Peter. "Perhaps I may be of assistance," he suggested tactfully. "Mr. Stocker attends this section. He designs jewelry, you know. Or were you thinking of something individual?"

He knew darned well that, in my best $59.95 gray herringbone suit, I wasn't thinking of anything more individual than the way I had my eggs for breakfast. But I surprised him.

"Yes," I said. "This is individual, personal and private and it'll interest him. Just say, 'Mr. Malone is here about the emeralds.' Got that? *The* emeralds. He'll know what you mean."

He was too well-bred and delicately nurtured to show patent surprise, though his eyebrows almost spelled out the word.

"Won't you have a chair, Mr. Malone?" he murmured. "It may be a few moments if Mr. Stocker is in the midst of an intricate drawing."

"He won't be in that much of a midst," I said and I put my hand in my pocket to keep from touching the short-barreled .38 I'd stuck in the waistband of my pants. He smiled again and walked gravely to the rear of the room and disappeared into the mahogany paneling, which must have been a door. When he reappeared a few moments later, there was a shadow of astonishment on his highbred face. This was probably a precedent.

"Mr. Stocker will see you, sir," he said.

He held the door open for me and unobtrusively faded away. Stocker's office, to my surprise, was a workshop; there were two Chippendale chairs and a small table with a leather top and ball-and-claw legs, but at the north window was a large tilted drawing board on which was thumbtacked a sheet of bluish tracing paper, and across the top of the board was a row of various colored inks in squat bottles and some pens and brushes, points up in what looked like an ordinary five-and-dime water glass.

The other night he had been very senatorial and suavely portly in white tie and tails, but today he had on the uniform—gray striped pants and the black jacket with a camellia in the buttonhole. He was very impressive at first glance, standing erect with his swept-back mane of Daniel Webster hair and wearing a dignified Congressional frown. But when you looked closer you saw his chin was just a pouchy, barbered flab, his mouth soft and fleshy, and though his eyes were normal enough, he gave you the feeling he was peering at you from behind a screen. But the round, modulated voice was straight from the rostrum.

And for all his impersonal front, I had more than a hunch he knew who Malone was. There was a kind of wariness in the air between us.

"I'm afraid you have me at a disadvantage, Mr. Malone," he said. "My associate mentioned emeralds but I don't understand. I can see you're not a client, if you'll pardon the observation, and well, there are simply no wholesale salesmen in our sort of business. Are you a newspaper reporter, by any chance? From time to time the *Courier-News* has printed special features in its Sunday magazine section. As you know, many precious stones—the larger ones, of course—have a romantic and oftentimes spectacular history, though I'm afraid the newspapers are inclined to overly sensationalize. I don't mean to criticize, however."

I'd walked in cold with nothing but the gun in my waistband, but he gave me the lead.

"I'm not a reporter exactly," I said. "I'm a staff writer for *Man's World*, the new magazine, and my editor—Charley Haas, he used to be with the *Saturday Evening Post*—wants to run a piece on emeralds with photographs, a full-page spread."

A creeping doubt began to see into his uneasy eyes. "Haven't I met you recently, Mr. Malone?" he asked. "It *is* Malone, isn't it. Joseph Malone."

That was a dead giveaway and I almost grinned into his face. Sure he'd met me the other night in the jostling lobby of the Esplanade House, but the introduction had been hurried and he couldn't possibly have remembered my name.

"No, no," I said. "The name's Maloney. John Vincent Maloney. I had a cover credit on *Metro* last month."

He said, "Oh," and some of the tension visibly went out of him. "What did you wish to know about emeralds, Mr. Maloney?"

"Well, something I could whip into an exciting yarn. Like the old Kohinoor diamond, for instance. That kind of thing."

"In that case, Mr. Maloney, I fear you'll find our

emeralds quite prosaic. All the famous ones are privately owned."

"To tell you the truth, I had a different angle. I want to start at the other end, how they come out of Colombia and all that."

Click—his eyes were behind the screen again.

"There's really nothing in that for you, Mr.—Maloney." Was his voice a little thicker or was I imagining things? "Government control has made the emerald trade very cut-and-dried."

This time I did grin at him. "Yes, I know. It's in the Book of Knowledge. But here's the story I have in mind—some emeralds are stolen, smuggled out of the country and I want to follow it step by step to the final sale of them in this country."

"But—that's impossible," he stammered. "Va-va-valuable stones have to be authenticated and dah-dah-documented. A reps—pardon me—a reputable jeweler, I mean reputable, would never under any circumstances handle a, well, let us call it an orphan stone of any worth. He would ha-ha-have to know the history."

"Sure," my grin spread deeply into both cheeks but it was all teeth and not even the embryo of a laugh. "A reputable jeweler, right. But the one I have in mind has a gilt-edged reputation though he's really as crooked as a snake climbing a corkscrew. He could get away with it. If they can counterfeit hundred-dollar bills so their own mother wouldn't know the difference, a forged document on a run-of-the-mill three- or four-carat emerald worth in the neighborhood of six to eight thousand dollars would be a pushover. And a high-class jeweler with top-price clients would stand to make a very solid profit, wouldn't he? I mean, you get stolen goods at, say, a tenth the wholesale, and then you don't pay any duty, so he could really clean up, couldn't he?"

Ah, I had picked the right one of the whole outfit

to work on. He was the weak sister, all front but baby mush inside—and the mush was oozing out of him in gray perspiration. He was trying desperately to hold onto that Senatorial façade but his face was all pouches and bags and quivering lips. He had relied so much on his reputation, Established 1887, he had never dreamed that he, of all the people concerned, could ever be suspected. And he must have known, he had to know, from the way I put it to him, hard and flat, that I wasn't talking about a hypothetical jeweler or hypothetical stones.

"No no no," he protested too hurriedly. "It's quite impossible. No one but a shay-shay—" that was a hard one for him to say. "Only a shady jeweler would dream of such a thing."

"Sure," I said softly. "That's what I mean, Mr. Stocker. A crook with an established honest front. In fact, the honester and reputabler he seems, the easier it would be. Right?"

"Really not, no, not in the least, not at all, really. A-a-an established man has too much at stake to risk his business for—for—for a few thousand dollars. You have the wrong notion entirely, Mr. Malone— Maloney, the raw-raw-wrong idea of how the jewelry business is conducted. The si-si-situation you describe is fantastic. A few thousand dollars, it really isn't very much, you know, it's nothing at all, really, I mean really, compared to the value of his good name. Ridiculous, you know, really ridiculous."

"Did I say a few thousand?" I purred like a cat with a fat, paralyzed mouse and that's always my trouble when I'm smarter than even myself. "It's a few thousand on each stone. Discounting the cost of the emerald, paying the hired help and, well, just general overhead, a six-thousand-dollar stone, retail, brings a net profit of around five thousand. Right?"

This wasn't wild guessing. It was well known that thieves got ten per cent or less for goods they had to fence. It had been printed over and over again in all kinds of magazines and books. In fact, last December I'd read a piece in a magazine called *FACT*. It was titled "Crime Doesn't Pay—Enough," and gave facts and figures on the average burglar's take to prove it. The writer had known his business and got it from the police and guys in jail. They got ten per cent—if they were lucky.

"Possibly but nah-not probably, Mr. Malone. It's—really too far-fetched, too far-fetched entirely, such a risk is absurd. The documents, you know, the documents. You can't ignore the documents."

"But I'm not, Mr. Stocker. Come to think of it, there's the whole point. Customers of a reputable but crooked jeweler would never question a document he gave them. But here's the kite-string link. Once the police got suspicious and started nosing around, this reputable jeweler would be up the creek, wouldn't he?"

He was gasping and sweating but I couldn't feel sorry for him. He'd gone into this for the same reason they all did—the quick and easy buck—closing his eyes to the dirty work involved. Still he was a pitiful remnant of the fine, prosperous figure he'd presented when I first walked in. You'd never have known him for the same man. He was baby mush.

A muted phone rang, the sound of it coming faintly from another room and he mumbled, "Excuse me a moment, Mr. Maloney," and fled from the office.

I was smug and I stood there with my hand inside my jacket around the scored handle of the gun in my waistband. I was doing fine. I had the right boy and he was going to pieces. All I had to do now was dangle his reputation, Established 1887, in front of him, mention Lieutenant Flavin and the police, and he'd give me the name I wanted. The name and place. Oh, the place, the place! I needed the place and he'd give it to me, I thought grimly, the gun fitting into the palm of my hand. When he came back, there'd be no more of this hypothetical stuff. I'd put it to him hard and straight.

I waited, soaking with anticipation in that high, stern joy which envelops you in moments of hard-won triumph. I waited.

I waited some more. The stern joy was beginning to slip a little, but I waited, watching the door through which he had gone to answer the phone in the other office—and suddenly I realized the phone was still ringing. Nobody had answered it and something fell out from under me. I took three long strides and flung the door open. The other office was empty. The something fell completely away from under me and I faced the fact that I had pushed Stocker too hard. He was gone, fleeing in panic to the boss on top the way a terror-stricken kid would flee to his father, and here was I with a gun and what could I shoot with it— pigeons? There were plenty of pigeons down in Military Park opposite Kresge's Department Store.

Oh, I'd been smart. And here I was in an empty office with nothing to console myself with but the thought that I'd outsmarted everybody, including myself.

Abe Kinney, that was the name that came into my mind, Abe Kinney, the other one, according to Flavin and Gilman, who'd been paying Janice Noonan's rent. Abe Kinney, the smart-money boy. Abe Kinney, who always had everything figured out. Abe Kinney, with enough money to throw a free party in the Esplanade House.

If only I'd thought of Abe Kinney sooner, I'd never have bothered with the soggy end of it—Stocker. Abe Kinney was the top and you had to go to the top to get anything done.

I walked out, nodded at the still faintly surprised clerk and caught a cab a half block down the street. I was beginning to feel as if I were living in cabs these days. Abe Kinney's apartment was on Clinton Street and I was there in ten minutes. I didn't take the elevator. Something was going to happen, possibly something violent and final, and the fewer people there were to recognize me, the better. I walked up to the top floor, paused a few minutes to get my breath because I wanted to be absolutely steady when the showdown came, then grimly knocked on his door, my hand around the gun under my coat. My knock was answered by a small, slight Filipino in a white jacket. Abe Kinney liked all the conveniences and comforts. Before the little Filipino could ask the question begun in his lifted eyebrows, I put my left hand against his chest, shoved him aside and walked in, growling, "I want to see Kinney." I saw him. He was sitting at the window in one of those extra modern chairs which look like a praying mantis. He had on a self-patterned dark-blue silk dressing gown and was wearing rimless glasses, reading the newspaper and sipping a cup of coffee. I got no more than a glimpse of his startled glance as I strode in, and then several things happened at once. The Filipino got my right arm in an excruciating judo hold from behind, another man savagely grabbed the gun, ripping two buttons from my coat, and a third man seemed to fall on me from the ceiling and something like a ball of iron hit me flush on the jaw and everything went up in a shower of sparks.

When I recovered consciousness, I was lying on the sofa and Abe Kinney, the trigger guard of my gun ringing his forefinger, was standing at my feet, looking as puzzled as was possible through his habitual sleepy expression.

"What the hell got into you?" he asked, more out of curiosity then from anger.

"You know damn well," I said, glowering.

He looked at someone behind me and shrugged. "All I know, Malone," he said, "is that you seem to have gone out of your mind."

"Do you want me to spill it in front of the servants?" I snarled. "I will but I don't think you'd like it."

"Oh dear, dear, dear." He sounded slightly amused. "This does sound serious, doesn't it? Do you mind stepping in the other room, boys? I think Mr. Malone and I will get along all right. At least, I hope so."

While the boys—and I should have remembered he always had some boys around him—marched out and closed the door, he pulled another of those odd-looking, modern insect chairs closer to the sofa and sat down, casually and unperturbed—though he stayed far enough away so that he was well out of range of any kicks I might throw in his direction.

"I don't understand this at all, Malone," he said conversationally. "We've always gotten along even when you worked for me and I know I'm not the easiest boss in the world. You must have quite a beef to come charging in here with a gun in your hand. It's not something which happens every day."

"No, it isn't, is it?" I said tightly, wondering if I could play the same trick on him that Bunny Riordan had played on me—kick the cocktail table in his face— but my luck was out there, too. The table was a sheet of plate glass the length of the sofa—ten feet—and it was held to a heavy, curlicued wrought-iron pedestal by four large neoprene suction cups.

"Or," he went on pleasantly, "perhaps I'm being stupid. Is there something I've overlooked? I don't recall your being a gambler and you've never tried to buck the wheel or the dice in my place, so you can't be sore about dropping your bankroll. The tables are honest, of course"—his smile was remotely mocking— "but that wouldn't make any difference to a poor, misguided sucker who'd just lost his all. You see, I'm puzzled. Thinking back, I remember you as always seeming rather easygoing and practical, which makes this—shall we call it a wingding?—all the more incomprehensible. But let's get down to the nut and nugget, Malone. What *have* I done to arouse you so, hm, impetuously?"

"I'll put it in one word," I said flatly, "Emeralds."

"Emeralds!" That did get a startled reaction from him. "What have emeralds to do with it? Or rather, what emeralds? Do you have some particular emeralds in mind?"

"Yes," I said, mocking now in return. "I have some very particular emeralds in mind."

"Well, I'll be damned," he said incredulously. He frowned and leaned a little closer as if to get a better view of my sanity. "Where do I come in? Am I supposed to have your emeralds or what?"

This wasn't going the way it should and a kind of dismay at possibly having made a mistake stirred inside me. But I was committed and had to keep going.

"No, you don't have them, but you'd damn well like to. Look—the sooner we cut out this double talk, the sooner we'll get it settled. One way or the other," I added harshly. "I don't have them and I don't know where they are and even if you shoved burning matches under my fingernails, you can't change that an inch."

"Burning matches! Do you know something? I think you're crazy."

"Oh sure," I said, attempting to work up a good healthy rage. "I'm stark raving mad. But I still have only to one o'clock."

He stared at me, narrow-eyed, for several seconds. "I've changed my mind," he said. "You're serious."

"What the hell do you think I am?" I flung at him. "Doing this for kicks? But why wait till one o'clock? It's going to be the same then as it is now. Get it over. See how much good it's going to do you. But I'm warning you—you're going to have to use that gun before you're done. I won't stand still for your goon squad, Kinney."

He got up, gave me a look, walked to the black plate-glass fireplace and stood with his back to me, snapping his fingers. Finally he turned.

"What's going to happen at one o'clock, Malone?" he asked quietly.

"How do I know? It's your idea."

He shook his head slowly. "Believe it or not," he said, "I haven't the faintest notion what you're talking about."

"And you don't know anything about Claire Loomis either, I suppose. But here's an angle you overlooked. I've been pushed as far as I'm going and I left a note for Lieutenant Flavin, homicide, Headquarters, and reported everything you said over the phone, word for word, including your threats against the girl. Maybe you can arrange an 'accident' for me, but not for both of us. If you don't let her go, it'll be the biggest mistake you ever made."

He frowned and his left hand clenched but relaxed with a gesture of negation. "If I didn't see how serious you are about this," he said, "I'd be sore. Now listen carefully—I didn't call you on the phone, I don't know the Loomis girl, and as for emeralds—damn it, what am I supposed to be up to?" he demanded angrily. "You come in with a gun, make threats, talk in riddles, and I still don't know what it's all about. In addition to that, I haven't the remotest intention of turning my goon squad, as you call it, loose on you. What do I have to do to make you believe me? Sign an affidavit, swear on a Bible or show you my honorable discharge from the Boy Scouts? I haven't made any mistakes, Malone. You're the one who's fouled up, and I'm sorry, and you can believe me when I say I wish I could help you."

By this time I, too, knew I was in the wrong place and had kept at him from sheer momentum. Also, I had to make sure, but this conversation would have been entirely different if he'd been the man I wanted.

"I need help all right," I said heavily, "But how can I get it if I don't know the score myself?"

"What is going to happen at one o'clock, Malone?"

I gave him a glittering grin and drew a finger across my throat. "Though it won't be as easy as that for them," I said. "I'm not a tied-up pig on a production line in a slaughter house. They'll have to work."

He pursed his lips. "I'd like to help you out but if it's as bad as you say, I don't want to get mixed up in it. I have impulses, but generally speaking I'm a cold son and I don't see any reason to change and, in my business, I have to look out for myself first, last and always. Why don't you go to the police? Even if it means a cell for awhile, anything's better than—what you just did."

"They've got the girl."

"The police have handled things like that before, too."

"Not the way this stacks up. At best, the police could grab only a few of the hired hands and I'm sure they'll have been told damn little. This is the same outfit that killed Harry Loomis and one more rubout won't mean a thing to them. Unless a miracle happens and I find what I'm looking for, nobody can help. Sorry I pulled that fuss on you."

"Forget it. Here—" He tossed the gun to me. "Regretfully, the most I can do is wish you luck. But I still think you should go to the police. They might just be able to figure something out for you. They're not stupid."

"I'd only make things worse for the girl. Maybe I'll be able to work something out."

Downstairs I didn't bother looking around for a cab.

I had run out of destinations. I walked, thinking furiously, but there was nothing new to think about and to go over the same old things would do nothing but defeat me. I had thought about them so much that they now seemed a tangle nobody could ever unravel. I walked clear over to the Passaic River and stood on the bank, somberly regarding the sluggish, oily flow of the polluted water. Even if I were the type to do the dutch—which I wasn't—I'd never have dived into that stinking sludge. A man would have to be at the lowest dismal point to go into that stuff for the last and biggest act of his life. Anyway, I was too raging to backfire into anything as flabby as suicide and it hadn't even been a passing thought.

It no longer made any difference that I'd drawn a blank on Alec Curry. He couldn't have done anything and if I told him the story, he'd have backed away fast, just like Abe Kinney but without being as polite. Alec bluntly and frankly looked out for number one a hundred percent of the time. "Sonny," he'd have said, "you're up against it for fair but I can smell a stink and I don't want to get it on me. You got yourself into it and you'll have to get yourself out of it and not get other people in trouble, too. No hard feelings, sonny, but when it comes to police and bloody murder you're on your own."

A million volts suddenly went through me and I stood up straight with a galvanizing jerk.

Sonny!

That was one of his pet words and the man on the phone had called me "sonny" several times … a whole avalanche of other remembered things swept over me. In talking, the man had used expressions you hear only in the ring or among fight people. Stumblebum, sneak punches, you're on the ropes, and from the way he said, "You're shifty, you're fast on your feet, always were," he definitely knew I'd had something to do with the ring. That fitted Alec to a T. I'd worked for him. I'd been a sparring partner in his own gym. He knew me and knew my style. And there was more, there was more. He was the one man who was in a perfect position to know people like Bunny Riordan, Harry Loomis and Garcia. They came to his gym, he talked to them, he knew what they were and how they could be used. He'd known Stocker the jeweler. He'd been in the same group around Janice Noonan on the opening night of the Esplanade House. And he had money, more than a sockful, plenty to finance an operation like this with the emeralds. And now, on the very day Claire was kidnapped, his gym was suddenly closed for repairs. The gym hadn't been closed for years. Alec hadn't closed it even when the rusty old iron plumbing flooded the locker room and the hall and a leak in the roof made a lake in one corner. When there was a buck to be made he wouldn't have closed the doors if the place had been on fire.

And now it was closed for repairs? Never.

His very offer of assistance assumed a new significance. He had never intended to help. He wanted to find out how much I knew and how deeply I was in it with Harry Loomis.

It all dovetailed, as I said, but you can't believe a thing like that all in one piece. You have to convince yourself bit by bit. I had known Alec for years, worked for him, liked him. He had a salty sense of humor and you never completely believed him even when he was being his most cynical and crabbed.

So it was impossible to grasp immediately that he wasn't what I'd thought him but somebody evil and conscienceless. I didn't fully take it in even with all the "facts" I'd assembled.

I had to hear it from him directly.

I went back to the gym. The same big ex-fighter was leaning against the building beside the door and now I was willing to give odds he'd been planted there to keep anybody from going in. Just to settle it in my mind, I walked over and noisily rattled the knob as if to break through the old lock—and sure enough, he gave me a truculent shove and said, "What's the matter, you can't read? See what it says? Closed for repairs."

"But I left a wrist watch up in my locker."

"Too bad. Come back Tuesday."

"It won't be there Tuesday. Somebody'll lift it. I paid fifty bucks for that watch."

"Then you're just horsed outta luck, bud. Closed till Tuesday."

"One of the plumbers can let me in, can't he? I want my watch."

"I'm telling you for the last time, bud, come back Tuesday. Now beat it."

"I want my watch!" I said, making a show of getting sore.

He planted himself in front of me and held a wide, broken-knuckled fist under my nose, scowling and wagging it to and fro. "What you want and what you get's gonna be two different things, bud," he said in his most menacing voice. "The joint's closed, see? Nobody goes up till Tuesday and that's orders. I ain't telling you again."

He didn't have to tell me again. He'd told me what I had to know. He was the downstairs watchman to keep people out and there was no need to ask why.

And there was Alec's failing, too, his penny-pinching miserliness, his using one of his cheap punchy bums for a job like that. I'd been there less than two hours before and he didn't recognize me. Nor did he seem to think anything of it when I walked into the building next door. He merely went back and leaned against the building again. Anybody whose brains were all there would have been suspicious immediately and given Alec warning.

The building I was in housed a machine shop, a printing outfit and an engraving plant, and with the hammer and bang of the machines, the rhythmic thunder of the big rotary presses and the screams from the trimmers and metal saws in the engraving plant, I almost reeled from the sheer physical battering against my ears. But ah, it was a Godsent bedlam! It would more than cover any noise I might make. But, more somberly, it also worked for Alec overwhelming all sounds in his place.

I went up to the roof. I met several people on the way up but, rushing around with fresh pink matrices, curved plates for the presses or wheeling metal tables with clean, silvery type in long galleys, they were too busy to give me a second glance. Alec's building was a whole story higher than this one but the top floor was vacant because of the rotting roof. The windows were boarded over but the nailheads I could see were crumbling with rust. All the same, it wasn't easy to pull that first plank off, having no real grip except with my fingertips. I was sweating when it finally wrenched loose with a screech of pulled nails and I had to sit on the edge of the skylight until my panting subsided. My hands were shaking from the unaccustomed strain on the forearm muscles. I do a lot of heavy lifting in my business but this was a different kind of exertion. Using the first plank for a crowbar, the next five boards came off easier. The window was nailed shut, but I knocked the glass out, hoping the din from the three floors below would smother the shattering crash, which sounded five times as loud as it probably was. I climbed cautiously into the empty gloom. The smell of wet, sealed-in ancient rot made my stomach turn and I tiptoed quickly across the spongy wooden floor to the door. The hallway was worse. It was darker than the inside of a whale and just as soggy underfoot. The downward steps had a limp give beneath me and twice I saved myself from breaking through by clutching the rickety handrail. Also, there was an entire step missing every here and there but I had thought of that and felt carefully ahead of me with my foot. I didn't dare flick on my cigarette lighter. The stench became less bad as I descended but I remembered how the gym itself used to stink, though it had been more bearably flavored with cigar smoke, sweat, liniment, rubbing alcohol and cuspidors. At least, that had been a familiar stink.

I must have picked the fire stairs—though God knows they would have been as inflammable as a haystack, if they'd been dry—for I was faced with a closed door when I reached the second floor. I had come down as slowly as a blind man but my heart was pounding and I was breathing heavily through my mouth. I looked at the closed door, which I could see dimly by the pencil-line of light from beneath it. It was an ordinary door over which sheets of galvanized iron had been nailed as a gesture in the direction of the fire inspectors. I wet my lips. If this were the usual fire door, it could be opened only from the inside. I wrapped my hand around the clammy knob and turned very slowly, possibly to give my breathed prayer time to work. I turned the knob as far as it would go before leaning against it. It stuck against the damp, swollen frame but opened finally with a tired whine when I put more weight behind the thrust.

I stepped swiftly into the hall—and directly across from me, not eight feet away, dressed (if you could call it that) in an old sweater and blue jeans, a big, thick-bodied man gaped incredulously, as if I were the ghost who lived in the foul den upstairs. In looks, he was almost the brother the one downstairs and his reflexes weren't any faster. He had just time for a flabbergasted "Hey!" before I was on him in one long stride with a straight hard right to the point of his chin. He fell back against the wall. I hit him twice again with everything I had and the second right hook felt like hitting a bag of sand instead of a solid jaw. He sagged and I caught him under the armpits before he could thud to the floor.

I was easing him down when the door opened and Alec Curry looked out. There was nothing wrong with his reflexes and he had a gun in his hand before I could drop my limp bundle and get at my own gun.

"Well, well, sonny," he said. "You're early but come in, come in. So much the less time we have to wait. *Come in!*"

There was nothing I could do. I let go of his unconscious watchdog and walked into the wretched little room he used as an office with him backing watchfully away as I came. Standing white-faced at the side of Alec's ancient golden-oak desk was Stocker. He also had a gun but looked ready to drop it and flee. Alec circled me widely and kicked the door shut.

"I see you don't have the package," he said sharply. "Or did you split it up and put it in your pockets? For your sake, sonny, I'm hoping that's the way it is."

"Where's the girl?" I asked.

He said, "Safe enough and far away, Mister Shifty," but there had been a brief flicker toward a second door at the side of the room.

"A girl?" Stocker stammered. "What girl? What's he talking about?"

"A girl," I said. "A hostage is a better word. Your friend here has gone into the kidnaping business along with everything else."

"There's no kidnaping involved," Alec snapped.

"No?" I looked at Stocker. "Take a peek at what's behind that door over there."

His face had been white but now it was green and he gasped, "Alec—"

"Shut your gob, dammit, both of you!"

"There's a girl locked up," I flung at Stocker, "and since the Lindbergh Law, kidnaping's the same finish as murder for all concerned. That's what you're mixed up in, Mr. Stocker. Do you like it?"

Alec's real viciousness was no longer hidden and he said harshly to Stocker, "Go downstairs and get Vince. We'll take care of Mister Shifty here in short order. He won't be so cocky when we get done with him."

"And keep right on going when you get downstairs,

Mr. Stocker," I said. "Keep going forever or you'll land with the rest of them. If you think they'll let me out of here alive, you're crazy. I know too much and—"

"Shut up!" Alec roared furiously.

I grinned thinly at him. "Shut me up," I suggested. "Go ahead. You've got a gun. Make me keep quiet."

He wasn't ready to shoot me yet and he was too smart to come close enough for me to get my hands on him. He could get at me through Claire but he hadn't thought of that yet and to keep him momentarily off-balance, I went on quickly. "Sure, send Stocker down for Vince but don't expect him back again. Take a look at him. He's ready to collapse. He peddled your hot emeralds, but when it comes to kidnaping and killing, he'll run to the police to save his flabby neck. Which would be the smart thing for you to do, Mr. Stocker. Thus far you're only a crook and the worst they can give you is a few years in jail, but if you stay with Alec, they'll give you the big one, the electric chair."

Stocker had been a sick man before but now he was coming apart and Alec flung him a savage glance of contempt.

"You stay here," he ordered, "and keep your gun on Mister Shifty while I get Vince. Aim for his belly."

I laughed. "And the minute you're out of the room," said, "I'll take the gun away from him and let him run down the back stairs. I'll let him get away. I don't have anything against him. It's a standoff, Alec. You can't trust Stocker, you can't shoot me down till you get the stones and you can't even yell for Vince, with the noise those machines are making next door. It's a standoff."

He crouched in such a height of driven fury that his mouth twitched like a madman's. "It's not such a standoff as you think, Mr. Shifty," he snarled. "I'm giving it to you in the belly and you'll live for days, screaming for a doctor and begging to tell all you know, just for a glass of water!"

He was in an unthinking frenzy and danced around on his skinny legs to get a frontal shot at me but I turned and kept my side protected with my right arm and left hand.

Stocker cried shrilly, "No, no, no!" and made a break or the door.

Alec pushed him back and yelled, "You're staying, damn you!"

Stocker staggered against the desk but, thoroughly terror-stricken, recovered and tried another rush for the door. Alec swore and hit him glancingly on the side of the head with his gun. He should have hit him again, knocking him out, for the jeweler's eyes had lost all sanity, but Alec turned the gun on me and snarled, "Stay where you are or—"

That was as far as he got. Stocker's first shot hit him in the shoulder and threw him against the edge of the desk. Holding the gun at arm's length in both hands, his mouth open in a soundless, lunatic scream, the fear-crazed man fired shot after shot and continued to pull the trigger even when the gun was empty. Alec was on his knees, swaying, his left hand clinging tenaciously to the desk. Stocker dropped his gun and, with a wild, inarticulate cry, plunged to the door, frantically fought it open and fled down the hall. Alec's gun was on the floor at his knees and I kicked it across the room before snatching up the phone and calling the police.

Alec had been shot five times, all in the chest area, and it was a miracle that he lived until Flavin and Gilman ran in ten minutes after the uniformed policemen from two prowl cars.

But Alec didn't soften in dying. His eyes blazed hatred through the pain. He knew he was going, but still he did everything possible to take me with him. He accused me of shooting him and killing Harry Loomis and at the very end, with death on him, he was gasping over and over, "He's got the emeralds, he's got the emeralds, he's got the emeralds...."

Flavin stood up and one of the uniformed policemen covered Alec with the threadbare rug.

"Well, that winds you up, Malone," said Flavin.

"Not quite," I said. "There's the gun on the floor. It's a nice shiny gun and I think you'll find Stocker's fingerprints all over it. And somewhere in the city, you'll find Stocker, too, probably hiding in his apartment. You won't have any trouble with him. He'll talk."

Claire was still behind that other door. I hadn't forgotten her but I didn't want her to see Alec on the floor with his blood on the rug, on his hands and on his twitching face where he had pawed himself. The memory of such a sight would be a long time fading and, frantic though she must have been, I had to spare her that last horror.

"There's a girl in that room," I said to Flavin. "It's Claire Loomis. Curry snatched her to get at me."

Someone gasped and two policemen flung themselves at the door. Behind it was a shallow closet and Claire was on the floor, bound and with a thick Turkish towel muffling her mouth. I had her in my arms before the police were finished cutting her loose. Her eyes were huge, her face drained, but she was not frantic and she clung to me, crying, "Joe, Joe, Joe!"

They had the decency to let her calm down before questioning her.

She confirmed everything I said about what had happened in that room and, at a curt order from Flavin, Gilman grabbed the phone and put out an alarm to pick up Stocker.

But Flavin didn't like it and he didn't like me. He was fair enough to say shortly, "And you're clear on the Loomis thing, too. Bunny Riordan died an hour ago with the fear of God in him and babbled it all to a priest. *After* we sweated him and I'll admit we mightn't have been able to do it without the things you told me.

But"—his jaw hardened—"you were still in it up to your neck and I'd give my right arm, my pension and ten years of my life to nail you for it."

"Nail me for what?"

"The thing you were after and got right in the beginning—that bundle of emeralds."

"I don't have them."

"You're a liar, Malone!" He'd have said it more strongly if Claire weren't there. "Man, you don't know what I'd go through to have a case against you that I could take to the prosecutor. By God!" he exploded, "It rips my guts to see a crook get away with a job like this. But you haven't gotten away with it yet, Malone. It'll be a long, long time before you can move those emeralds and maybe you'll never move them. I never give up, remember that. Remember it every time you try to get rid of those stones. But I want you to try, Malone. That's what I'll be waiting for."

"There's nothing to wait for," I said, but without hope of convincing him. "I don't have them."

"And in the meanwhile you'd better memorize every law in the books, plus the ones that go back to Fourteen Ninety-two, because you won't be able to turn around without being picked up. I'm going to make it so miserable for you that you'll wish you were under that rug with Curry. And moving away won't do you any good. There'll be police wherever you go and we'll be in touch with them. You've got a sweet life ahead and I wouldn't be in your shoes for a ton of emeralds."

They took us to Headquarters and it was another two hours of answering questions and signing papers before they let us go. I felt no joy. Claire took my arm.

"It's over, Joe," she whispered. "It's all over."

I said, "Yeah."

"Are you worrying about what that Lieutenant Flavin said?"

Worried? No, I was more bitter than worried. If I took Claire out for an evening or for a drive, somewhere along the line there'd be a cop to yell at us and badger us and take the fun out of it and if I got really serious about her, how could I ask her to marry me and have to take it with me?

"Can—he really make that much trouble for you, Joe?" she asked.

"No," I lied, so she wouldn't worry. "He might bother me for a little while but they've got too much other work to keep it up for long. Can I buy you a drink?"

"I really don't want to go into a bar, Joe. I—just want to be alone some place."

"Okay. I'll take you back to your hotel."

"I mean with you, Joe. Unless you'd rather be by yourself."

"No, no, let's ..." Let's what? I'd be doing her a kindness to send her away before Flavin's campaign started on me, but I couldn't do it so abruptly. And I did want to be with her. For a while, anyway. "How's about my apartment?" I said. "We can have a quiet drink and listen to the radio and talk and later on broil a steak or something." At least there wouldn't be any cops in the apartment.

"I'd like that, Joe," she said.

I got my car from the parking lot and drove to the apartment. I stopped at the mail box in the lobby. I hadn't looked at my mail or even thought of it for the past few days, and the little box was filled with bills, advertisements and the usual junk. As I pulled them out, a buff-colored slip the size of a postcard fluttered to the floor. I bent over and picked it up. It was a notice from the post office that they were holding a package which had been too large for my box. I didn't realize for a minute. I hadn't ordered anything and wasn't expecting any packages—and suddenly there was a kind of roaring in my ears and I began to shake.

From a long way off I heard Claire say anxiously, "Joe, Joe! what's the matter, Joe?"

"A phone," I said. "We got to get to a phone right away. I have to call Flavin. Where's a phone?"

I ran out to the sidewalk and up to the store on the corner. It was closer than my apartment. I couldn't stop shaking but did manage to dial Flavin.

"It came in the mail," I yelled at him. "A card. I got it right here. It was in my box."

"What the hell are you talking about?" he snarled.

"This card. It's been there, in my mailbox. A card."

"Make sense, will you?"

I gripped the phone and took a breath. "This card," I said as slowly as I could. "It's from the post office. They're holding a package there for me."

He said, "What!"

"They're holding a package in the post office for me," I repeated. "And you're coming with me. I'm not going alone or—"

"Where are you now?" he interrupted.

"At my apartment and—"

"Wait for me."

Claire and I waited on the corner, not holding hands but gripping hands. Flavin and Gilman were there in fifteen minutes. We got in the back and I handed the card to Flavin over the seat. He nodded and put it into his pocket without saying anything. There was a line at every window in the post office, but we went around back and Flavin gave the card to the postmaster, who sent one of the clerks running to get the package. The four of us stared blankly when he returned.

It wasn't a package. It was a cocoanut, carved and painted to look like a head. Flavin swore and glowered at me.

"Way-way-wait a minute," I said. "They sell these at the Canal, the natives, they paddle out in canoes and sell these, they make them themselves—"

Flavin grabbed it from the clerk and shook it. There was no sound from inside. He held it over his head and hurled it down on the cement floor. It bounced and rolled under a table.

The postmaster said calmly, "Get the fire ax, Walter," and looked curiously at the addressed tag which was tied to the cocoanut head. "One of my clerks must have made this out. That's George Singleton's handwriting. Just a minute—"

The next few minutes were the most confused and incredible I'd ever spent. The one clerk came running with the fire ax and Gilman split the head open with two blows and inside was a wad of absorbent cotton. Flavin opened them on a bench and there wasn't a word spoken when we saw that heap of emeralds, green fire under the electric lights. Then Gilman whistled and Flavin whispered, "No wonder, no wonder ... Good God, there isn't a one under three carats!"

By this time Singleton, the other clerk, had come up and Flavin was all cop again, sharply motioning me to silence.

"Do you remember who mailed this thing?" he asked, showing Singleton the cocoanut head.

Singleton was a very serious young man and he frowned. "If you mean did I know the man, no," he said with exasperating care.

"What did he look like?"

"Well—he was a big man, bigger than usual. He was extremely drunk and that's why I made out the mailing tag for him."

"Jeff Buckley," I breathed. "So he was telling the truth when he said he *had* to get it to me."

Flavin said, "Be quiet," but the edge had gone out of his voice. Then to Singleton, "Do you remember any more?"

"No-o, that's about all. He had the address on an envelope and mumbled something about his boss getting mad at him. He paid the postage and left."

There was nothing much left to say after that. Flavin could now see that Jeff Buckley hadn't known what was inside the cocoanut, so Buckley and I couldn't have plotted anything and Harry Loomis had used both of us.

Flavin took me aside. "I never apologized to anybody for doing my job," he said in that abrupt voice of his, "and I'm not going to start now. But if you happen to park in the middle of Broad and Market Street at high noon in the middle of a parade, I'll kill the ticket for you. Does that satisfy you?"

"The world is full of dumb Micks," I said, "so why should we be different, either of us?"

"Why don't you take your girl out and buy her a cocktail or are you going to drag her around with cops for the rest of her life?"

Outside, I said happily to Claire, "He said to buy you a cocktail."

Her hand was in the fold of my arm. "But I told you where I wanted to go, and why," she said. "We almost got there the first time and I think we should try again. Now how did you say it was going to go? You were going to make a drink and we'd sit and listen to the radio and talk and after awhile we're going to broil two steaks—or did you change your mind?"

I laughed out loud right there on the sidewalk. "I don't have a mind, honey. All I've got up there is a great big rosy cloud. But why are we standing here? I thought you wanted to go to my apartment and have a drink and listen to the radio and—"

People stopped and looked at us. I didn't blame them. Nobody stands in the middle of the street laughing the way we were unless he's out of his mind....

THE END

Larry Holden was born Lorenz F. Heller in West Hoboken, New Jersey on October 5, 1910, studied journalism at Rutgers and worked on various New Jersey newspapers. He then ran away and became an able seaman on a freighter before jumping ship and returning to start writing fiction. Heller published his first novel,  *Murder in Make-Up*, in 1937 and continued to write under a variety of names, including Laura Hale, Larry Heller, Lorenz Heller and Frederick Lorenz, working with publishers like Pyramid, Popular Library, Beacon and Eton Books. He also wrote TV scripts under the name Burt Sims. As Larry Holden he turned out three crime novels in the 1950s and nearly 100 stories, several of them featuring private eye Dinny Keogh. Heller eventually settled in the Venice, Florida area, where he supported himself entirely on his writing. He died on December 12, 1965.

Larry Holden Bibliography
(1910–1965)

Novels:
Hide-Out (Eton, 1953)
Dead Wrong (Pyramid, 1957)
Crime Cop (Pyramid, 1959)

Stories:
...And Death Makes Ten (*Detective Tales*, June 1947)
Another Man's Poison (*Shadow Mystery*, Apr/May 1948)
Any Corpse in a Storm (*Dime Mystery Magazine*, Aug 1949)
Anybody Lose a Corpse? (*Mammoth Detective*, Aug 1946)
The Big Haunt (10-Story Detective Magazine, Oct 1948)
Blackmail Means Homicide (*15 Story Detective*, Feb 1950)
Blood Money (Suspect Detective Stories, Nov 1955)
Bloody Night! (*Dime Mystery Magazine*, Oct 1949)
Bodyguard (*Thrilling Detective*, June 1951)
Bullets for Beethoven [Dinny Keogh] (*Mammoth Mystery*, June 1946)
Coffin Key (*Detective Tales*, Oct 1951)
A Corpse at Large (*Ten Detective Aces*, July 1949)
Corpse in Waiting (*New Detective Magazine*, Nov 1950)
A Corpse to His Credit (*Dime Detective Magazine*, May 1947)
Criminal at Large (*Suspense Magazine*, Summer 1951)
The Crimson Path (*Detective Tales*, Sept 1947)
Cry Murder (*New Detective Magazine*, Oct 1952)
The Crying Corpse (*Ten Detective Aces*, Sept 1948)
Death Brings Down the House (*10-Story Detective Magazine*, Apr 1948)
Death Carries the Mail (*F.B.I. Detective Stories*, Aug 1950)

Death for Two! (*Detective Tales*, Dec 1952)

Death in Dirty Linen (*Shadow Mystery*, June/July 1947)

Death in Six Reels (*Doc Savage*, July/Aug 1948)

Death in Thin Ice (*Shadow Mystery*, Feb/Mar 1948)

Death Is Where You Find It (*Suspect Detective Stories*, Nov 1955)

Die, Baby, Die! (*Detective Tales*, June 1948)

Don't Crowd My Shroud (*10-Story Detective Magazine*, Dec 1948)

Don't Ever Forget (*Detective Story Magazine*, Mar 1953)

Don't Wait Up for Me (*Triple Detective*, Fall 1955)

The Eighteen Screaming Corpses (*Detective Tales*, Jan 1948)

The Expendable Ex (*Dime Detective Magazine*, June 1952)

Face in the Window (*Detective Tales*, June 1951)

Fall Guy (*Detective Tales*, Aug 1953)

Forger's Fate (*Dime Detective Magazine*, Apr 1951)

The High Cost of Chivalry (*Dime Detective Magazine*, Dec 1951)

Home for Christmas (*Thrilling Detective*, Dec 1947)

House of Hate (10-Story Detective Magazine, Apr 1949)

Humpty-Dumpty Homicide (*Detective Tales*, June 1949)

If the Body Fits—(*Dime Mystery Magazine*, Dec 1947)

If the Frame Fits—(*Detective Tales*, Dec 1951)

I'll Be Home for Murder! (*Detective Tales*, Apr 1948)

I'll See You Dead! (*Detective Tales*, May 1947)

In Her Mother's Best Bier! (*Detective Tales*, Dec 1948)

Keeping Honest (*Doc Savage*, Winter 1949)

Kickback for a Corpse (*All-Story Detective*, Apr 1949)

Killer's Kiss (*Detective Tales*, Aug 1949)

Lady in Red (*Detective Tales*, Oct 1948)

Lady-Killer (*Dime Detective Magazine*, Dec 1952)

Lethal Boy Blue (*Detective Tales*, May 1949)
Love Me, Love My Corpse! (*Detective Tales*, Aug 1948)
Make Mine Mayhem (*New Detective Magazine*, Jan 1949)
Man with a Rep (*Detective Tales*, Dec 1949)
Mayhem at Eight (*New Detective Magazine*, May 1950)
Mayhem's Mechanic (*Detective Tales*, Sept 1946)
Morgue Bait (*New Detective Magazine*, Dec 1951)
Murder and the Mermaid (*Dime Detective Magazine*, Oct 1952)
Murder Never Gets Too Old (*Private Detective*, Jan 1950)
Never Dead Enough (*New Detective Magazine*, Sept 1947)
Never Turn Your Back (*Mike Shayne Mystery Magazine*, July 1959)
Nightmare (*Detective Tales*, Oct 1952)
No Dead End (*Triple Detective*, Spring 1955)
On a Dead Man's Chest (*Thrilling Detective*, Apr 1953)
One Dark Night [Dinny Keogh] (*Mammoth Mystery*, Dec 1946)
One for the Hangman (*Suspect Detective Stories*, Feb 1956)
Operation—Murder (*F.B.I. Detective Stories*, Aug 1949)
Orphans Are Made (*Mobsters*, Feb 1953)
Out of the Frying Pan... (*15 Mystery Stories*, Oct 1950)
Port of the Dead (*New Detective Magazine*, July 1947)
Prelude to a Wake (*Dime Detective Magazine*, Feb 1952)
Red Nightmare (*Dime Mystery Magazine*, July 1947)
Sailor, Beware! (*Detective Story Magazine*, May 1953)
Save Me a Kill (*New Detective Magazine*, June 1953)
Self-Made Corpse (*Detective Tales*, Apr 1949)

She Cries Murder! (*New Detective Magazine*, June 1952)

Sing a Song of Murder (*Dime Detective Magazine*, Aug 1952)

Snow in August [Dinny Keogh] (*Mammoth Mystery*, Aug 1946)

The Spice of Death (*Private Detective*, Dec 1950)

Start with a Corpse [Dinny Keogh] (*Mammoth Mystery*, Jan 1946)

There's Death in the Heir [Dinny Keogh] (*Mammoth Mystery*, Aug 1947)

They Played Too Rough [Dinny Keogh] (*Mammoth Mystery*, Mar 1946)

This Shroud Reserved (*New Detective Magazine*, Oct 1951)

Those Slaughter-House Blues (*Mammoth Detective*, Feb 1947)

A Time for Dying (*Dime Detective Magazine*, Aug 1951)

Too Many Crosses [Dinny Keogh] (*Mammoth Mystery*, Feb 1947)

Tragedy in Waiting (*Invincible Detective Magazine*, Mar 1951)

The Trouble with Redheads (*Mike Shayne Mystery Magazine*, Apr 1959)

Two-Headed Killer (*15 Mystery Stories*, Feb 1950)

Undressed to Kill (*New Detective Magazine*, Sept 1949)

Vicious Circle (*Detective Tales*, Nov 1949)

The Voice That Kills (*15 Mystery Stories*, Aug 1950)

Wake of the Ermine Chick (*15 Story Detective*, Dec 1950)

When Cops Fall Out (*Detective Tales*, June 1953)

With Hostile Intent (*Fifteen Detective Stories*, Dec 1954)

With Love and Bullets! (*Detective Tales*, Feb 1953)

Written in Blood (*Ten Detective Aces*, May 1948)

You Can't Live Forever (*New Detective Magazine*, Aug 1952)

You Die Alone (*Fifteen Detective Stories*, Oct 1953)

You'll Die Laughing (*Detective Tales*, Oct 1950)
You're Killing Me (*Detective Story Magazine*, Sept 1953)

As Frederick Lorenz

Novels:
A Rage at Sea (Lion, 1953)
Night Never Ends (Lion, 1954)
The Savage Chase (Lion, 1954)
A Party Every Night (Lion, 1956)
Ruby (Lion, 1956)
Hot (Lion, 1956)
Dungaree Sin (Chariot, 1960)

Stories:
Backbite (*Justice*, Jan 1956)
Big Catch (*Justice*, July 1955)
Living Bait (*Justice*, May 1955)

As Laura Hale

Novels:
Kiss of Fire (Rainbow, 1952; reprinted in Australia as *Kiss Of Death*, Phantom, 1953)
Woman Hunter (Falcon, 1952; reprinted in Australia, Phantom, 1953)
Wild is the Woman (Rainbow, 1951)
Lovers Don't Sleep (Falcon, 1951)
Desperate Blonde (Beacon Australia, 1960)
Lessons in Lust (Beacon, 1961)
Sensual Woman (Beacon, 1961)
The Zipper Girls (Beacon, 1962)
The Marriage Bed (Beacon, 1962)

As Larry Heller

Novels:
I Get What I Want (Popular, 1956)
Body of the Crime (Pyramid, 1962)

Story:
Blood Is Thicker (Guilty Detective Story Magazine,
    Mar 1957)

As Lorenz Heller

Novel:
Murder in Make-Up (Messner, 1937)

Stories:
Blood Money (Suspect Detective Stories, Nov 1955)
A Tasty Dish (Suspect Detective Stories, Feb 1956)
Twilight (Short Stories, Nov 1956)
The Hero (Mystery Tales, Dec 1958)
The Last Hunt (Adventure, June 1959)

As Burt Sims

Television Scripts:
1953: "Death Does a Rumba" (Season 2, Episode 12,
    Boston Blakie)
1953: "Island of Stone" (Season 2, Episode 1,
    Chevron Theater)
1954: "Tailor-Made Trouble" (Season 1, Episode 11,
    Waterfront)
1956–1959: Seven episodes of *Sky King*
1958: "Beautiful, Blue and Deadly" (Season 1,
    Episode 14, *Mike Hammer*)
1958: "Texas Fliers" (Season 1, Episode 18, *Flight*)

Black Gat Books

Black Gat Books is a new line of mass market paperbacks introduced in 2015 by Stark House Press. New titles appear every three months, featuring the best in crime fiction reprints. Each book is size to 4.25" x 7", just like they used to be, and priced at $9.99. Collect them all.

1 Haven for the Damned
by Harry Whittington
978-1-933586-75-5

2 Eddie's World
by Charlie Stella
978-1-933586-76-2

3 Stranger at Home
by Leigh Brackett writing as
George Sanders
978-1-933586-78-6

4 The Persian Cat
by John Flagg
978-1933586-90-8

5 Only the Wicked
by Gary Phillips
978-1-933586-93-9

6 Felony Tank
by Malcolm Braly
978-1-933586-91-5

7 The Girl on the Bestseller List
by Vin Packer
978-1-933586-98-4

8 She Got What She Wanted
by Orrie Hitt
978-1-944520-04-5

9 The Woman on the Roof
by Helen Nielsen
978-1-944520-13-7

10 Angel's Flight
by Lou Cameron
978-1-944520-18-2

11 The Affair of Lady
Westcott's Lost Ruby /
The Case of the Unseen Assassin
by Gary Lovisi
978-1-944520-22-9

12 The Last Notch
by Arnold Hano
978-1-944520-31-1

13 Never Say No to a Killer
by Clifton Adams
978-1-944520-36-6

14 The Men from the Boys
by Ed Lacy
978-1-944520-46-5

15 Frenzy of Evil
by Henry Kane
978-1-944520-53-3

16 You'll Get Yours
by William Ard
978-1-944520-54-0

17 End of the Line
by Dolores & Bert Hitchens
978-1-944520-57

18 Frantic
by Noël Calef
978-1-944520-66-3

19 The Hoods Take Over
by Ovid Demaris
978-1-944520-73-1

20 Madball
by Fredric Brown
978-1-944520-74-8

21 Stool Pigeon
by Louis Malley
978-1-944520-81-6

22 The Living End
by Frank Kane
978-1-944520-81-6

23 My Old Man's Badge
by Ferguson Findley
978-1-9445208-78-3

24 Tears Are For Angels
By Paul Connelly
978-1-944520-92-2

Stark House Press

1315 H Street, Eureka, CA 95501 707-498-3135
griffinskye3@sbcglobal.net   www.starkhousepress.com
Available from your local bookstore or direct from the
publisher.